THE CLUE OF THE
LINOLEUM LEDERHOSEN

**DON'T MISS ALL OF
THE PREVIOUS BOOKS
EVER PUBLISHED IN THIS
THRILLING SERIES!**

Whales on Stilts

M. T. Anderson's Thrilling Tales

THE CLUE
OF THE
LINOLEUM
LEDERHOSEN

M. T. ANDERSON

Illustrations by **KURT CYRUS**

HARCOURT, INC.

ORLANDO   AUSTIN   NEW YORK
SAN DIEGO   TORONTO   LONDON

www.HarcourtBooks.com

Illustrations copyright © 2006 by Kurt Cyrus
Cover illustration copyright © 2006 by Tim Gabor

Library of Congress Cataloging-in-Publication Data
Anderson, M. T.
The clue of the linoleum lederhosen/by M. T. Anderson.
p. cm.
"M. T. Anderson's Thrilling Tales."
Summary: Looking forward to a vacation, Katie, Lily, and Jasper attach their flying Gyroscopic Sky Suite to the Moose Tongue Lodge and Resort, where they mingle with other child heroes found in books, and where they become embroiled in a mystery involving lederhosen-clothed quintuplets and a screaming ventriloquist.
[1. Mystery and detective stories—Fiction. 2. Hotels, motels, etc.—Fiction. 3. Resorts—Fiction. 4. Humorous stories. 5. Mystery and detective stories.] I. Title.
PZ7.A54395Clu 2006
[Fic]—dc22 2005020752
ISBN-13: 978-0-15-205352-9 ISBN-10: 0-15-205352-2

Text set in Stempel Garamond
Designed by April Ward

First edition
A C E G H F D B

Printed in the United States of America

*This book is dedicated
to the loneliest whale*

(SEE APPENDIX A.)

THE CLUE OF THE
LINOLEUM LEDERHOSEN

Summertime Tantrum

"Great scott!" cried Jasper Dash, Boy Technonaut. "Your mother just lost her hand in the rotating band saw!"

Katie Mulligan kept dribbling her ball of wastepaper back and forth between her knees. "Uh-huh," she said. "Sure."

Katie's mother screamed and held up her bloody stump.

Katie kicked the ball of paper into the trash basket, scoring two points. She asked, "Right at the wrist?"

Jasper rushed to Katie's mother's side. "Don't you worry, Mrs. Mulligan!" exclaimed Jasper. He grabbed her arm. "Lie down flat while I prepare a tourniquet."

They were in the Mulligans' garage, watching Mrs. Mulligan make a roulette wheel for the Salvation Army's charity casino—or at least that's what they'd been watching until Mrs. Mulligan's gruesome accident.

"Where do you want to go to dinner?" Katie asked her friend Lily.

Lily shrugged. When she was alone with her friends, she was very quiet, hiding behind her bangs, watching rather than speaking. She was naturally pretty shy. She was also made bashful by the sight of industrial accidents, even though she knew that Katie's mother was just playing a prank on Jasper, the way Mrs. Mulligan always did. Run over by a moose, decapitated by the dryer, burnt to a crisp by a defective AM/FM clock radio—there was no tragedy too weird and stupid for Jasper to believe.

"Don't you worry, Mrs. Mulligan," he was saying. "By next Thursday I'll have you fitted up with a bionic hand that will be every bit as good as your old hand. And it will have extendable fingers and photon thrusters, and there'll be a space in the thumb to conceal your cyanide pill and lock-picking tools."

Mrs. Mulligan stopped screaming. She looked at him skeptically. "My lock-picking tools?"

"Or whatever," said Jasper. "Whatever's small and can be concealed in a secret chamber."

Mrs. Mulligan took off the fake rubber arm stump and stretched her fingers. "Why would you possibly think I would want lock-picking tools?"

"Ah," said Jasper, somewhat displeased. "I see you are not actually wounded at all."

"Who has *lock-picking tools*?"

"Mrs. Mulligan, was your accident with the band saw just a jolly prank to 'put one over on me'? Because if it was, may I—ma'am—may I say that I did not entirely appreciate the humor."

"Jasper, do you have lock-picking tools? What do you kids *do* all day?"

"Good question," sighed Katie. "It's vacation, and we're bored out of our minds."

Mrs. Mulligan waved her rubber wrist in the air. "Well, that's why I was trying to cheer you all up a little."

"By sawing off your own hand?" said Jasper.

"You girls didn't even jump," said Katie's mom.

"Because we see it all the time," said Katie. She groaned, "Aaaaaaallllllllll the tiiiiiiiiiiime." She let her tongue hang out of her mouth and her head roll back.

Katie Mulligan lived in Horror Hollow, a small, eventful suburb where there were constantly problems with phantasms, murderers, door-to-door tarantula peddlers, and slime. She even had her own series of books written about her. They told every gory detail of how she fought off ghouls on the rooftop, bats in her bedroom, and wyverns in the den. It was a popular series, since she was the only girl heroine to fight evil in flip-flops. Katie was plucky and brave and always spoke her mind.

Unfortunately, in order to have lots of "cliff-hanger" chapter endings in the Horror Hollow series, a lot of tedious cliff-hanger things had to happen to the family in reality. But even a family constantly attacked by living dolls and ferocious skate-punk vampires couldn't have disasters every minute of their lives. There had to be some time in between disasters for eating, drinking orange juice, and walking the dog. This meant that in order to provide excitement before the real action started, they had to play a lot of stupid, disgusting pranks on each other. That got old very quickly. There are only so many times you can watch your father's face melt before you want to just say, "Okay, stop the bus." It makes you almost long for the moment when, finally, the pine tree out the window grows a big spindly claw and the adventure starts for real.

Jasper also had a series written about him, but it had been written many, many years before. In his series he invented stupendous devices and went on startling adventures where there was plenty of action and fisticuffs. Unfortunately, the Jasper Dash, Boy Technonaut series was no longer read very much, except by kids with the influenza, after they'd run out of everything else to read and had watched a couple of days of MTV, even the reality shows about sorority girls basting turkeys with hard liquor. Once flu victims had played all the Chinese checkers they could stand with their brothers and had used the Internet to look up scenes of ape-to-ape violence, then, sometimes, they would read and enjoy a good, clean, fast-paced Jasper Dash adventure that had been sitting in their attic for forty years. They would like the Jasper Dash series, but often the scenes they really remembered from his books, the ones that really stayed with them once they got well, turned out to be things they'd dreamed when they fell asleep in the middle of Chapter 12.

Often, if you go to a town library and under Keyword Search type "Jasper Dash," you'll come up with a list of his books—and beside each one, it says: "Withdrawn. Withdrawn. Withdrawn. Withdrawn." This means that they are no longer in circulation. Some librarian has taken them off the shelf, wiping away a tear, and has opened the book to the back, where there's a pouch for a card dating back to the time of the Second World War, and she'll crumple up the card, and then she and her fellow librarians will take special knives and slice away at the book and will eat the pages in big mouthfuls until the book is all gone, the whole time weeping, because they hate this duty—it is the worst part of their job—for here was a book that was once someone's favorite, but which now is dead and empty. And the little cheerful face of Jasper Dash, heading off to fight a cattle-rustling ring in his biplane, will still be smiling pluckily as they take their Withdrawal Knives and scratch his book to pieces.

Lily did not have her own series. She didn't

realize yet how exciting her life really was. Her friends knew, because she had often gotten them out of scrapes, but she didn't believe what her friends told her. She thought she was just the quiet sidekick.

Want to learn more about these fascinating characters? You can read their previous book, *Whales on Stilts,* available for the laughably low price of $15.00 at fine bookstores near you.*

"If you're bored," suggested Mrs. Mulligan, "why don't you get out of the house? You could go down to the old swamp, or the rust exhibit at the museum, or maybe that weird store that just appeared last night on Bunk Street."

"No," said Katie. "I'm sick of adventures. I'm sick of it all."

Mrs. Mulligan put her hands (intact) on her

---

*Remember: If you buy two copies and hold them at different distances from your eyes, you can see the book in 3-D.

"I built my house out of *Whales on Stilts,*" says David Gonzales of South Rupture, Indiana. "I stacked them up in a big pile. I've never regretted it. It was way cheaper than marble."

hips and smiled. "Whenever I hear that, I know a particularly big and baffling adventure is just around the corner! You kids just wait!"

Katie gritted her teeth. She was about three inches away from having a good old-fashioned tantrum. "No," she said. "I'm going to have a normal vacation. Like a normal kid. Not like a mass-market celebrity in a weird, psychopathic suburban development." She stood up and began rummaging around in the garage mess. She knelt in front of a pile of stuff. She started to rifle through it. She grunted, "We're going to play Twister. Okay? That's it. We're playing Twister."

She threw old kites and skates and carpet samples across the garage.

"Hey!" said Mrs. Mulligan. "Katie! Stop!"

Jenn Ross of Dexter Heights, South Dakota, writes that *she* uses multiple copies of *Whales on Stilts* to keep deer out of her flower garden. "Oh, I love that book," she says. "It's just the right weight for hurling. Or I use a kind of a book launcher my husband made for me. Yessiree Bob, there's many a deer in Dexter Heights that regrets it ever heard about the exciting career of plucky heroine Lily [Gefelty]."

Katie didn't listen. She hurled a pair of running shoes onto the hood of the car. She tossed a map of the world into the air.

Lily felt kind of embarrassed for Katie, in that tingly way you feel embarrassed when a friend is having a tantrum in front of you and you're not along for the ride.

"Katie!" scolded her mom.

Katie kicked a box of Christmas lights under the workbench.

"Be reasonable," said her mother.

Suddenly Katie shrieked and leaped back.

"Jupiter's moons!" gasped Jasper Dash. "Your father's dismembered torso!"

FATHER'S TRUNK

"Oh, *that* old thing!" said Katie's dad, strolling in from the den.

Katie's mom laughed. "Oh, Ben! The torso! I haven't seen that for years!"

He smiled. "Not since the day of our wedding."

They squeezed each other and giggled.

"That's it," said Katie. *"I'm through!"* she screamed. "Forget it!"

And by three o'clock that afternoon, she, Jasper Dash, and Lily Gefelty were whizzing off for a week of rest and relaxation in the mountains at the Moose Tongue Lodge and Resort.

A Room with a View

Jasper had wanted to go to the Moose Tongue Lodge and Resort for a long time. There were trails through the mountains and decks you could sit on and look across the horizon. Jasper had a way of finding places that looked like they had never seen 1968, let alone 1973 or 1994.

Plus, he had recently received a coupon for a free dinner in their dining room.

Katie, Lily, and Jasper didn't have the money for hotel rooms, so Jasper had fired up his Gyroscopic Sky Suite, which was designed to attach inconspicuously onto the outer walls of classic hotels.

Inside, there were several small rooms with bunks, each room equipped with a shortwave radio and a speaking snorkel. There was a lot of closet space and a common area for sitting together and playing games. The Sky Suite also had other things one might need when on vacation, like a sauna and a crime lab. The whole capsule was shaped kind of like a rocket, but it was shingled so that when it attached itself to a vintage hotel, it appeared to be a turret. It had rocket engines, like almost everything Jasper invented, but they were only for emergencies. Usually, it was dragged through the sky by a robotic jet with a large girdle. The Sky Suite hung below the jet. The robot drove.

During the flight up to the lodge, the kids sat in Lily's room, playing 52-pickup with magnetic cards. Occasionally, they'd look out the window and see the foothills flying past beneath them, covered with oaks and maples.

Finally, the lodge itself came into view. They saw the mountain, its summit bristling with weather antennae. It was nestled on cliffs below the mountain peaks. It was surrounded richly by pines—a huge wooden hotel with gables and chimneys and grand staircases and big windows

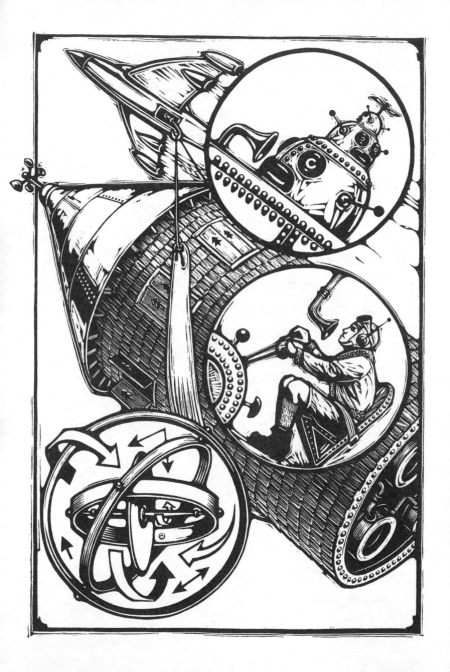

and little suspended bridges that led into the woods across fissures.

Jasper lifted his speaking snorkel. "All right!" he said. "Aim and toss!"

The robotic jet pilot said, "Righto! Hold on to your lunches!"

"Huh?" said Katie. "We already ate our—"

Suddenly the pilot ejected the Sky Suite from its girdle. It flew through the air. With a huge crash, it hit the side of the hotel. As it hit, big metal clamps bit into the wood—there was a detonation—loud as the blasting of volcanoes—and the Sky Suite was secured, smoking, looking as if it had always been there.

It took a minute before anyone could hear again.

"Jasper!" said Katie, livid. "That was insane!"

Lily bit her lip and waited for the police to arrive, banging on the metal door of the capsule. But there was no sound.

"Have no fear, chums," said Jasper. "We've arrived as safe and sound as chicks on Easter

Sunday." He unstrapped himself from his chair. "I just hope we managed to connect with a hallway. Otherwise, it could be a little bit sticky."

The three of them walked to the metal door. Jasper unlocked the door and swung it open.

They stepped out. They were in a guest's private bathroom. A man was cowering in the bathtub suds. There were broken wooden planks and chunks of plaster floating on the gray water all around him.

Jasper cleared his throat and said, "I'm sorry. You appear to be in our antechamber." He marched to the bathroom door.

Katie gasped, "Oh wow. Oh wow. Here, let me help you pick up some of this . . . Oh, I'm so sorry. I'm so . . ." She and Lily scurried around, gathering pieces of wood.

The man made a high-pitched meeping noise.

Jasper said, "Madam, we regret any inconvenience we may have caused you. Unfortunately, we're staying right here in rooms 23A–E."

He pointed at the metal door of the capsule, on which was painted "ROOMS 23A–E."

"This is the fourth floor," whispered the man. "I think you have the wrong room."

"Excuse us, good lady, if you will," said Jasper. "We have to go tip the concierge. He appears to have given us a smashing view of the hot spring."

Jasper walked out through the man's bedroom and into the hall. The girls followed him.

"Jasper," said Katie, "Jasper, you idiot! How are we going to get back to the capsule? We'll have to go through that man's bathroom every time we want to go to our bunks!"

"What man?"

"The bald one in the bath."

"I would hate to inconvenience anybody," said Jasper, "except that I've found, in certain situations, that people would rather have a good story to tell than just another dull old bath. I think that eventually he will see the funny side of it."

"After a few days?" demanded Lily.

"I hope it doesn't take him that long," said Jasper, uneasily. "He might find it hard to sleep until then. The ventilators are quite loud."

They walked down a sweeping staircase into the lobby.

The lobby was cavernous. On the walls were old moose-hide snowshoes and wooden skis. There was a birch-bark canoe hanging above the front desk. A row of mounted animal heads hung high on the wall. People were bustling everywhere. Porters were taking bags; bellhops in pillbox hats were squeaking, "Yes, ma'am!" and bowing; there were lots of big men in raccoon-skin coats and pinstripe suits smoking cigars and pointing at portraits on the walls. The

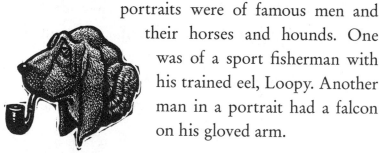

portraits were of famous men and their horses and hounds. One was of a sport fisherman with his trained eel, Loopy. Another man in a portrait had a falcon on his gloved arm.

Jasper walked right up to the front desk.

"Hello," he said. "We're Jasper Dash, Lily Gefelty, and Katie Mulligan. We've just taken those rooms in that new tower addition, rooms 23A–E, off the bathroom of 46B."

"Oh, Mr. . . . Mr. Dash? *The* Jasper Dash? Boy Technonaut?"

Jasper looked humbly at the inkwell. "Yes. Yes, that's me, sir."

"It's great to meet you!" said the man at the desk. "We just cleared a whole bunch of your books out of the lounge library! Burned a whole stack of them!"

"Ah," said Jasper, looking at his toes.

"Hey, you aren't the only child hero at the hotel this weekend. We got the Cutesy Dell Twins, the Manley Boys, and those adorable mystery-solving Hooper Quints! You know, the Quintuplets!"

"Ah," said Jasper. "The Manley Boys used to babysit me."

"The Manley Boys?" said Katie, standing

behind him. "You know them? They look really cute in their books."

"They are not so cute," said Jasper miserably, "when they have covered you with lye and buried you in the victory garden."

"Oh," said Katie. "Sorry. If it means anything, I'm not crazy about the Cutesy Dell Twins being here."

Lily explained to Jasper, "They go to our school."

"They're like two little love-struck pythons," said Katie. "With, you know," she stuck out two fingers near her mouth like fangs. "Mean and bitey," she said.

Jasper explained to the man at the desk, "We have come to redeem our coupon for a free dinner."

"A free dinner?" said Katie.

"I always try to be frugal when I travel," said Jasper, "as well as clean and well mannered." He pulled out a photocopied coupon for a free dinner. "I received this last week."

The man at the desk looked at it. "Eh, nah,"

he said. "No. Nope." He handed it back. "Not real."

"What do you mean by 'not real'?" asked Jasper.

"This isn't from us."

"Then who is it from?"

"Why would I know?" asked the man at the desk.

Katie pressed, "Who would send us a fake coupon to your restaurant this weekend?"

"That's not something I know," said the man at the desk. "But whoever they are, they sent out a bunch of them. Like to the Cutesy Dell Twins." He pointed over Jasper's head.

"Oh, thrills," grumbled Katie.

"Oh *look*!" came a little blond voice. "It's *Katie* and her friend . . . that friend who's *with* her. That *girl.*"

Lily frowned and went off to inspect some prints of hound dogs.

The voice was, of course, one of the Cutesy Dell Twins. One was blond and the other was brunette. They came up to Katie looking tan and like their hair had just been dipped in movie popcorn butter.

"It's so *great* you're *here*," said a Twin.

"And who's your *friend*?" said the other, blinking admiringly at Jasper.

He was a bit intimidated and said nothing.

"Does he have *issues*?" asked the first Twin, hopefully.

"Katie," said the second one, conspiratorially. "Have you seen the *Manley Boys*?" She took Katie's arm. "They're around here somewhere. They're the well-built sons of ace detective Bark Manley. More than once a baffling crime that's had him stumped has been solved through the resourcefulness and ingenuity of his two boy heroes."

"Most recently," said the other Twin, "*The Clue of the Wiggling Rock.*"

"The clue was solved by them," explained the first Twin. "And the bad guy is totally in jail!"

"They are so handsome," said the second

Twin, "that it makes me feel like there's a net over my brain."

"*Whoppa cute.*"

"Whipple-triple-decka cute."

"Cute that's *bona fiiiiide.*"

The Twins nodded in unison.

"Okay. Have fun!" One of them winked at Jasper. "Nice to meet ya!" she said. "Hope we'll see ya around!"

They walked away, giggling and looking back at the Boy Technonaut.

"What strange young women," said Jasper.

"Just wait till they've got their fangs in you," said Katie. She called over to Lily, "The coast is clear."

Lily came back over. She mumbled, "I was looking at the menu."

"I don't like the Twins, either," said Katie. "They talk about people behind their backs."

"Shall we go for a hike before it gets dark?" said Jasper. "I'll get a trail map."

"We need some water," said Katie.

"I've got a water bottle back in my room," said Lily.

Jasper said, "Why don't you just pop up and—"

There was a commotion near the front door. A man ran in screaming.

"They've been kidnapped!" he yelled. "They're gone!"

"Who?" yelled someone convenient.

"The Hooper Quints! All five of them! They're all gone! Someone took them!"

Five Go Missing

The crowd of people in the lobby of the hotel was clamoring for more information. The hotel manager rushed over. "Slow down!" he said to the distraught man. "Tell us slowly what happened!"

"I'm a cabdriver, see? I was hired to bring them adorable mystery-solving Hooper Quints up to this swanky hotel here. I packed 'em all into the car and started up the mountain. About two miles from here, there was some wise guy standing in the road. He held out his hand for me to stop. I stopped and rolled down the window and asked him what the matter was. He said I had something stuck to the front of my car. I asked him what. He said, 'A big . . . thing.'

I said could he be any more, you know, precise, and he went, 'It's gray.' I said, 'What? Like smoke from a bonfire?' and he said I was on the right track, that it was gray *like* smoke from a bonfire, but, he had checked, and it was *not* smoke from a bonfire, and I better get out and look at it.

"I asked him could he maybe give me another clue. He tried doing this, you know, charade, but he wasn't very good at it, so it was just a kind of twisting motion with his waist and then this little hop, with his elbows out. I asked him whether that was an imitation, and he shook his head no and kind of tugged at his ear, meaning, '*Sounds like* the *name* of what's on your front bumper.' I asked him was it alive, and he said, 'No. Um, yes. Yes. Yup, it's alive. You better get out.' So. Then I got out and went around the front of the cab and didn't see anything on my front bumper, and suddenly— *ka-powee*—he jacked me in the back of the head with something heavy. I fell down to the ground and passed out. When I woke up, the Hooper Quints were all gone from the car."

"Completely gone?" said the hotel manager.

"And here's the weirdest thing," said the cabdriver. "*There wasn't really any living gray thing on my front bumper at all.*"

"Yeah," said the hotel manager sourly. "That's uncanny."

A woman called out, "The Hooper Quints could be in great danger!"

"We'll get a search party of guests together," said the hotel manager. "We'll scour the woods." He looked at the crowd. "Who wants to volunteer?"

Almost everyone raised their hand. He began breaking them into groups so that they could go separate ways.

"I refuse," said Katie, "to be a part of this right now. We're here on vacation from crime solving."

Jasper had his hand up and was bobbing up and down on his tiptoes.

Lily's hand was raised halfheartedly. When she saw that Katie wasn't volunteering, she said, "Shouldn't we help?"

"I'm not getting sucked into this whole Quint thing," said Katie.

Jasper said, "We may be their only hope."

Katie crossed her arms. "Us and the other seventy-five people in the lobby."

"Frankly, Katie," said Jasper, "I'm a little disappointed."

"You two go on the wild-goose chase," said Katie. "I'm going to go sit on the veranda and read. It's a vacation. I'm relaxing."

The hotel manager cupped his hands around his mouth and said, "Everyone who wants to help with the search, move outside!" The crowd moved to the door.

Katie, trying to seem nonchalant, said, "Okay. Really. You two have fun. I'm going to go read a magazine."

"Are you sure?" asked Lily.

"Later," said Katie.

Jasper shook his head, frowning in disapproval.

Katie forced herself to ignore his expression. He had no right, she thought, to look at her like that. She was just taking an afternoon off.

She smiled tightly and said, "Tell me all about it later!"

The lobby was almost empty. Waving, Jasper and Lily turned and followed the rest of the crowd outside.

Feeling a little empty herself, Katie watched them go.

Stop worrying, she thought. *They'll find the Quints without me.*

And, indeed, the search was on!

THE SEARCH IS ON!

If you've ever solved a mystery at a luxurious resort before—you know, firing your pistol off the ski lift, recording the muttering of counterfeiters by the pool, climbing over the roof in a catsuit, discreetly picking poison blow darts out of your neck in the Krakatoa Lounge—if, for a moment, you think back to the last time you solved a mystery in a resort setting, you'll know that this is the point in the game when you really need to start looking for suspects. I will parade a bunch of highly suspicious freaks past you, and you will have to ask yourself:

1. Did they have a **motive** to commit the crime? In other words, do they have a reason for doing the deed?

2. Did they have the **opportunity** to commit the crime? Do they have an **alibi**?

3. Did they have the **means** to commit the crime?

Also, keep your eyes open for things that might make people look suspicious. Sometimes a little subtle detail that might escape you at first turns out to be the thing that really matters most. For example, docs a particular character carry a sword? Does a particular character wear a Halloween mask the whole time and breathe in a rasping sort of way? Does a character walk on all fours, bobbing his head up and down? Does a character suspend you over a pit of lava and say, "Soon it will all be mine! Mine! Mine, I tell you!"? In the difficult world of police detection, it's often little clues like this that give the game away.

Now, it has to be said, clues like this still would have been completely mystifying to the Manley Boys. Jank and Fud Manley could not have been stupider if they had been made out of margarine.

"We'll find those Quints," said Jank, squinting into the sun. "It's a cinch."

"I hope they're still in their box," said his brother Fud, who had missed the explanation of what a "quint" was. He thought they were something like a wrench.

The search parties were gathered outside the hotel on the grass in the middle of the circular drive. Above them the flag flapped in the summer breeze. The crags of the mountain rose all around them.

The hotel manager called out, "Now, first. Identification. Does anybody know what the Quints look like?"

Nobody said anything.

All sorts of guests had turned out for the search. Some were in wet bathing suits and some were in fancy linen suits. Some wore tweed hiking gear. Some were in evening gowns or black tie. Lily was in jeans and a sweatshirt. Jasper, needless to say, was in shorts and kneesocks.

"Would somebody who has read the Quints'

books please give us a description?" the manager requested.

Nobody said anything.

"Who here," he asked, "has read one of the Quints' books?"

The wind blew high above them all, ruffling a bored eagle's wings.

"The books came out a really long time ago," said someone apologetically.

"Are the Quints the ones with all the weird machines?" someone else asked.

"No," the first person answered. "That was . . . uh . . . What was that stupid kid's name? I read those books when I was a boy . . . Something like Hopalong Jack, Young Hypernaut, or, eh, Jack Sprint, Child Techno—"

Lily yelled out quickly, "Maybe you have one of the Quints' books in the hotel library!"

The manager nodded. He sent one of the bellhops back into the hotel to check the library for Hooper Quints books so the group could hear them described and get a positive ID.

"Lily," whispered Jasper, "do you think that man might have been talking about me?"

"No," said Lily. "No way." She squeezed Jasper's shoulder, but she didn't look in his eyes, because she was lying.

"Do you think no one reads my books anymore?" Jasper asked.

"I read them," said Lily. "I've read them all three times."

"You're Jasper Dash, Boy Technonaut?"

Lily and Jasper turned to see who had spoken. It was a boy in overalls.

"Indeed," said Jasper.

The boy stuck out his hand. "I'm little Eddie Wax. Remember me?"

Lily and Jasper looked mystified at Eddie Wax. They had never met him before. He was red haired and wasn't wearing any shoes. He had filled the bib pocket of his overalls with trail mix.

"Yep," said Eddie. "Picture me about five feet higher? With a horse's head? And the rest of the horse?"

Lily and Jasper still had no idea who he was.

"You know, from the horse books. Eddie Wax! I rided Stumpy. In *Stumpy Rides to Glory.*"

Lily nodded, smiling. "Oh, sure. I did a book report on *Stumpy Rides to Glory*!"

"Yep. I'm Stumpy's rider. Stumpy is my series."

Lily looked confused. "I, um, I only remember the first book."

"Yep, I'm Stumpy's rider." Eddie nodded and waved his hand in the air, saying, "For that whole series, I was. Yep, she's a good horse. Good, sweet horse."

"Are you sure there was—"

"Gentle as a luna moth and brave as a grizzly in the Coldstream Guards." Eddie looked upset, and his voice had that weird, embarrassing gluey quality that voices get when we're trying to pretend we're not about to cry. "She's a good horse, Stumpy. Best horse anyone could ask for."

"Attention!" cried the hotel manager. "We

found one of the Quints' books under the player piano in the hotel library."

"Read it to us!" an older woman in pearls and a broad straw hat beseeched him. "I do so love a story!"

"Okay, okay. If you'll all sit down for a second, I'll read you the description of the Quints from the beginning of the book. Will that work?"

They all sat down, and waiters walked between them, handing out sandwiches and bottled lemonade.

The hotel manager opened to the first page of *The Hooper Quints on an Oil Derrick; or, The Danger Gang!* and he began to read.

The HOOPER QUINTS on an OIL DERRICK;

or, THE DANGER GANG!

By
EDNA G. SLATTERMEYER

CHAPTER I

Jolly Derrick!

*D*ERRICK!" said Ray Hooper. "Jeepers-to-crow, an oil derrick is the perfectest place to spend our holiday!"

"Yes," said La Hooper, "I've always wanted to gad about on an oil derrick! If I couldn't have come, I would have broken my fingers! Come, let's run and play dress-up near the extraction pipes!"

"Such larks!" exclaimed Doe Hooper, swaying by one arm from the scaffolding. "I can almost see slag from here! This will be the best holi—"

"Sid, duckie," said the woman in the wide straw hat to the hotel manager. "Maybe skip to the next page?"

"Ah yes. Thank you, Mrs. Mandrake." The manager flipped to the next page. He scanned it, looking for clues of the Hoopers' appearance. "Aha," he said. "Here's where the Hooper Quints are first described." He looked around the crowd. "Pay close attention," he said.

The Hoopers were all quintuplets. They had been born all together! That's why they got along so well. They did everything together! They went on picnics and solved mysteries together. Recently, they had solved a mystery of a big hard old cake in *The Loud Ratcheting Noise (Hooper Quints No. 42)*. They also solved mysteries on farms.

They had a nanny! She was a musical nun. She was always there to give them sandwiches and ginger beer when they were hungry. She was a fun nun! Once, when they were very poor, she made them little matching suits out of the living-room curtains. That was great fun! When the curtain pants wore out and the shirts got torn, she cut the linoleum on the kitchen floor into lederhosen.

She also taught them how to sing. She gave each one of them the name of a note. That's where their nicknames came from! Doe! Ray! Mi! And so on all in a row! Would you like to hear them sing?

No, you wouldn't. They were awful! It was kind of a joke that the nun played on them. She told them they had beautiful voices, but they sounded really bad. They—

Sid stopped reading, shut the book, and shook his head. "I can't go on," he said. "I just can't. Anyway, you get the idea."

Everyone agreed he shouldn't go on.

"Wow, that was...um...," Lily commented quietly to Jasper. "That explains why no one has read the Hooper Quints' books. I feel really bad for them."

"Oh, the book wasn't so terrible," said Jasper. "I liked the plucky high spirits of the narrator. I always enjoy exclamation points."

The hotel manager passed out paper place mats with a map of the mountain and advertisements for local businesses. He divided everyone up into search parties. Lily and Jasper, unfortunately, were split up. Jasper looked sad; he had been put in a group with the Manley Boys, who had always made fun of him when babysitting. Lily, meanwhile, ended up in a group with Eddie Wax and a man in a green poplin jumpsuit. She would have felt much better with Jasper around. She was always nervous with new people.

"We could ask to be switched into each other's group," said Lily.

"No," said Jasper unhappily. "A good citizen does not ask for special treatment."

"I bet the hotel manager wouldn't mind."

Jasper shook his head. "I don't want to be one of *those* people." He pointed over at the pearled and hatted Mrs. Mandrake, who was following the hotel manager around and asking him questions loudly.

"Sid? Will there be bears? One can't stand the shagginess of their muzzles."

"No bears, Mrs. Mandrake."

"Will we be late for dinner?"

"I can't say, Mrs. Mandrake."

"Oh and, Sid? Sid, will the priceless Mandrake Necklace be safe in my room? My late husband gave it to me. I didn't want to wear it outside for fear the dazzle would stupefy the dogs."

The manager had clearly about had it with Mrs. Mandrake. "Yes, Mrs. Mandrake. It will be fine in your room. You're going with that group," he said, pointing to Lily, Eddie Wax, and the man in the green poplin jumpsuit. "Does everyone have a map of the mountain? And everyone knows where you're going?"

Everyone said "Yes" or "I guess so."

"Has everyone gone to the bathroom?"

People shuffled their feet and looked embarrassed. "Go on," said Sid. "Go on!" Many of them headed inside.

"I'll be back in a tick, Lily," said Eddie Wax, jerking his thumb toward the lodge. "Right after I done nature's business."

"See you, horse kid," said the man in the green poplin jumpsuit. He did some stretches, picking up his knee and clenching it in his arms. "I'm Rick," he said to Lily. "I don't need the bathroom right now, because I've taught myself the art of self-control."

"I'm Lily," she said. "I'm glad you . . ." She didn't really know how to finish the sentence.

"Yup. Me, I'm staying out here in the sun and the fresh air," said Rick. "Can't shake your hand because I have my knee in my arms."

Lily nodded. She did not like small talk very much. She never knew what to say, and that made her feel kind of dull, even though it shouldn't have. People who are really good at small talk are sometimes a little suspicious, because they're so smooth. Especially in a mystery novel.

Rick was not all that good at small talk. "I'm standing on one leg," he said, "and what's wrong with that?" He bounced up and down. "Let's get going!" he said. "Let's truck! Where's the horse kid? I want to get a move on! Let's find those Quints!"

"Poor little things," said Mrs. Mandrake, adjusting her hat.

"I hope they're safe," said Lily.

Mrs. Mandrake said, "Indeed."

The Quints, however, were not doing well at all.

Quints in Darkness

"Ow," said La Hooper.

"Double ow," said Ray Hooper.

"You're kicking me," said La.

"I can't see anything," said Doe. "It's dark."

And dark, my friends, it was.

"Jeepers-to-crow," said Ray, "a bandit's cave in the mountainside is the perfectest place to spend our holiday!"

"Doe?" said La. "Kick Ray."

Doe tried. No luck.

"We could sing to lift our spirits," one of them suggested.

Believe me, you want me to end the chapter now.

Sin and Soufflé

Katie, meanwhile, wandered alone through the corridors of the hotel. She passed identical doors. The knuckles of her hand brushed each doorframe, as if she wanted to knock.

She couldn't go back to her room, 23C, because her room was inside of someone else's bathroom, and she didn't have the key. She frowned. This was exactly the kind of problem you had to expect when you traveled with Jasper. Something crazy always came up. Katie was tired of crazy things.

She passed a small lounge where some little kids were sitting around an entertainment specialist from the hotel. The entertainment specialist leaned toward the kids and spoke to them in a breathy, hushy voice. "There's a story," the entertainment specialist said, "that this hotel is *haunted*. Do you want to hear it?" The kids clapped their hands and shouted.

Katie snorted and walked on.

No more ghosts.

The woman looked after her. "Don't snort at the supernatural," said the entertainment specialist. "It can hear you snort."

It can hear me do a lot of things, for what I care, thought Katie. *I am ignoring ghosts. I am ignoring missing quints. I am going to pretend everything is normal. I am going to go down to the gift shop and buy the new issue of* Snazzy, *and I'm going to sit on the veranda with the sun shining on me and I'm going to read. And no dark shape is going to cover up the sun, and nothing on the veranda is going to drip blood, and the faces of girls in the magazine aren't going to whisper my name and ask for help, and I am just going to have a good, quiet time. So there!*

She went down the main staircase. She looked around the lobby. *That's funny . . .*, she thought. There was a row of mounted animal heads, and it looked like two were missing.

She curled her fists up into balls, muttered to herself, "Out being cleaned," and walked right past. She was not going to be delayed by a couple of missing heads. There was relaxing to do.

She went into the gift shop. They had key chains, batteries for cameras, aspirin, and plush goats. They also had a rack of books and magazines. She spun the rack to hide several Horror Hollow books against the wall. She found *Snazzy.* ("Coolest Summer Clogs!" "Connect the Dots: Spread Freckles to Other People!" "Is Your Guy Also Luggage? One Girl Speaks Out.")

She put the magazine on the counter. "I'd like to buy this," she said, and took out her wallet.

Nothing weird or supernatural happened. She put down her money, and the salesclerk took it. He gave her change. She thanked him and went to find someplace to sit.

There was a beautiful view from the porch she found. It was up on the third floor, overlooking the front lawn. The sun was high and it fell through the forests that covered the steep sides of the mountain. Far below her, she could see other blue peaks. Cars crawled up the mountain road far below, swiveling around switchbacks. Kids were jostling each other in the rumble seats.

On the front lawn, the guests stood around in their search parties and waited while a few stragglers went to the bathroom or bought sunblock. Katie resolutely didn't look for her friends in the crowd.

She put on her sunglasses and sat back in a deck chair. She opened the magazine on her lap. The pages fell wide to several cards scented with perfume. She took them out and held them close to her nose. Each one smelled good. On her favorite, there was a picture of a handsome, sweaty man with uneven hair, a pout, a corduroy jacket, and a black eye. It was called "Tainted: A Fragrance."

She sat for a while, looking out over the landscape. She thought about how Lily couldn't understand that, sometimes, Katie just wanted to be a *girl*. She didn't want to lay demons to rest or talk about how great it would be to bring back a live pterodactyl. She just wanted to think about boys. She wanted to be pretty. She knew the teen magazines she read were sort of stupid; that was why she read them. It was fun. She laughed at them herself. But all the same—what was wrong with being silly once in a while? What was wrong with laughing and trying something new with your image? For once, when she did her hair nicely and then went to hang out at Jasper's, she would have liked to have Jasper and Lily say, "Hey, Katie, your hair looks really nice," instead of "Whoa. That's going to get really messed up when you put on the mind-meld helmet."

Though she didn't like to admit it, sometimes Katie was a little embarrassed by Jasper and even Lily. She couldn't imagine what some of the kids at school would say if they ever met Jasper.

She particularly wondered what some of the boys on the soccer team would say.

There was one soccer player in particular that she had a crush on. His name was Choate Brinsley. He had the most perfect oval-shaped face. That was something she couldn't talk about with Lily. Lily would just get uncomfortable. Lily didn't like to admit that people had faces or bodies at all.

Katie leaned back in her chair and daydreamed about kissing Choate Brinsley after a game. It would be raining, and their hair would cling to each other. She would move her lips across his cheek. His shin guards would nuzzle her ankles. And he would say:

"Now—to seize that diamond necklace and make good my escape!"

Katie's pupils suddenly snapped back into focus.

The gruff voice had come through the window

beside the porch. Katie listened carefully. "It's got to be in here somewhere." It was a man's voice—someone muttering to himself.

But no. No! Not her business. She'd quit. No more mysteries. Katie scowled and stared down at her knees.

The voice said, "The priceless Mandrake Necklace will soon be mine. Mine, mine, do you hear me?" It was a man's voice, sort of grating, a little bit like the voice of an assistant manager in a second-rate electronics store that specializes in phone adapters. Katie ignored it.

There was a crash as something in the room was dropped.

Katie, unconcerned, flipped a few pages of *Snazzy.* "Is Your Date a Creep or a Keeper? 17 Questions to Help You Think."

She heard dresser drawers being slammed and suitcases being overturned. She heard underwear flying through the air.*

She read, "*Question 3. **Slick or slouch?** Is he*

---

*It sounded silk.

52

polite with your parents, or does he just mumble a few words and try to crawl out the basement window? A. Yeah! B. No way! C. . . . "

Behind her the man growled, "Could it be hidden in the . . . No . . . No, it isn't . . . Could it . . ." The thief was ripping the pillows apart, by the sounds of things.

Katie read that ingredient *numero uno* for gals in clogs in the modern era was a sinful smother of antioxidant-enriched body soufflé applied liberally to the feet and ankles.

"I must find it quickly!"

Katie read an article on ski pants.

"Could it be that the old bat stuck the necklace in the . . . Aha! Yes!"

The thief laughed heartily.

Katie dog-eared a page recommending citrus juice to freshen up dimples.

"Bingo!" cried the thief.

She heard a door slam.

She didn't move a muscle.

She turned the magazine sideways to admire a model's boot-cut wet suit.

She heard the porch door open behind her.

She angrily flipped to the table of contents and began looking for the article on the mono-brow.

Suddenly there was a piercing scream. A bloodcurdling scream, right behind her.

Katie dropped the magazine and started to her feet.

She didn't make it to a standing position, however, before she was engulfed—a man in a black cape fell upon her, and she tumbled back-ward, now screaming herself . . .

THE SCREAMS OF A SPECIALIST

Katie struggled with the cloaked man. She kneed him in the gut. He wheezed and rolled off her. She sprang up and prepared to fight. He was still lying on the deck.

He was an old man with white hairs growing out of the top of his nose. He wore blacked-out round glasses and a black cape. He tried to raise himself up on one arm.

"I'm—*hunh*—I'm terribly sorry, miss," he said, addressing the door. "It appears we are all in a heap."

"What are you doing?" Katie demanded.

"Professor Nerwald Schmeltzer," said the old man, feeling for the railing, grasping it, and heaving himself to his feet. Katie stepped forward and gave him a hand. "Bat specialist," he said, shaking her hand. "It is my lot to admire the bats."

Now that he was on his feet, he carefully fixed his pearly-white bouffant hairdo by touch. He said, "You appear to be startled."

"You screamed."

"Bats navigate by sound."

"What?" said Katie.

"I find my way around as the bats do— echolocation. I am the next stage in man's evolution. I shriek and listen to hear the contours of objects. I caress the world with my voice. It is a quaint and frivolous habit that shall one day prove to be mankind's salvation."

Katie looked at him suspiciously. "You really can tell where to go just by screaming?"

"Indeed," said the old man. "I have come up to the mountains to study the squeak of the Ghost-Faced Bat in the caves hereabouts."

Katie didn't really believe him. "So when you screeched," she said, "you were just trying to see me?"

The professor suddenly started and Katie heard a thump—someone was trying to slip by in the hallway on the other side of the door. The thief!

She ran past the professor into the hotel. She could hear someone fleeing down the hallway. She scrambled after him.

The professor followed. Katie heard a series of bloodcurdling yelps as he listened his way down the corridor.

She paused at an intersection of hallways. She didn't know which way the thief had gone.

She had just enough time to realize that she had accidentally started to solve a mystery, and to think, *Darn it! I don't want to*— when suddenly the professor crept up by her side.

"Are you chasing someone?" he whispered.

"Yes," she said. "Unfortunately."

"Who?" he asked.

"A thief," she said.

"Aha," he said.

She said, "*Shh.*"

For a moment they were quiet. They could

hear the air conditioners in people's rooms and someone vacuuming.

Then she heard it—someone padding quickly down one of the corridors. She couldn't quite tell what direction it was coming from or how far away it was. She shut her eyes and—

AAAAA
AAAAR
RRRRRR
RRHHH

She was flattened against the wall.

"Sorry," said Professor Schmeltzer. "Just checking to hear if my belt buckle was tarnished." He leaned down and polished the buckle with his handkerchief.

Katie's ears rang.

He said, "I find the mountain air corrodes metal more quickly, even, than the vapors near the sea."

She listened. Nothing. The thief was far away by now.

"Thanks," she said. "Thanks a lot."

"For . . . ?" asked Professor Schmeltzer.

"Never mind," said Katie, stomping away from him.

She disappeared down the corridor.

"Ah, impetuous youth," said Professor Schmeltzer.

He lifted up his dark glasses and watched her retreat. He smiled to himself.

Then he put away his handkerchief and, without making a noise, walked back to his room to read the paper.

Suspects on Parade

The forest smelled sweetly of pine needles. The trees sparkled in the sun. Lily, Mrs. Mandrake, Eddie Wax, and Rick walked down a steep slope toward a stream. In the woods Lily could see little benches on little side paths. There were places where people had tied Chinese lanterns to branches. In the evening guests could stroll out from the hotel veranda and walk through the woods. The forest would look soft and haunted. People could talk about the things that were important to them, like hope or sadness or their families.

Lily wished that she were with her friends. She wished they were all doing this together. When you are with your friends, even chores can seem like fun. Once, for example, some friends of mine and I tried to lift up the sinking city of Venice on concrete pilings. Dave nearly dropped the cathedral of San Marco on Chloe's leg. Man, we laughed so hard, we almost spat out our snorkels. We still tease him about that occasionally. It was one of the happiest days of my life.

Lily felt uncomfortable about how things were turning out. Katie was sitting by herself somewhere. Jasper—poor Jasper—was off with the Manley Boys, who were probably being mean to him.

Sometimes Lily worried about Jasper. He was a little too good for this world. Even though he usually was the one protecting her with his ray guns and his atomic cannon, sometimes he was the one who needed protecting. She wanted to put her arm around his shoulders and tell him that everything was fine, that he was a good person and it didn't matter what people said about his belief that the world was hollow or about the antennae on his bike.

Instead, she was walking along beside Eddie Wax, who was nice but who wouldn't stop talking.

"Yep, Stumpy and me won the Portertown Derby. Mayor of Portertown turned bright red as a roadhouse borscht and threwed his hat right on the ground. Guess you know that, if you read the book. The wind was blowing up through my hair. It was blowing it back kind of heroic. Like this." He held up some of his hair. "Hey. Lookee here. Like this. Wind. And Stumpy, Stumpy was . . ."

Lily had imagined the vacation working out very differently. She wanted Jasper, Katie, and her to be walking together through these woods, talking about school and movies, with the lights sparkling in the trees, and people whispering secrets to each other, and the fountains lacing the evening air with water.

"They said I couldn't do it, but I showed them I could," said Eddie Wax. "I gentled Stumpy, I took her in the race, and I won first place, fair and square. They said I couldn't, but I did. The prize was a pie so big, I swum in it for a week."

Rick called back, "Hey, you two getting to know each other? That's cute."

He and Mrs. Mandrake waited by a turn in the path for Lily and Eddie Wax to catch up. Lily was relieved. Rick had never appeared in a book. He was just staying at the hotel. He seemed a little boastful, but Lily thought he might be less peculiar than some of the other guests, a little more straightforward. She gladly joined him, and the four of them walked together down the path.

Rick was busy trying to impress Mrs. Mandrake. "You psychic?" he asked. "I'm psychic. I can move things with my mind. I just don't do it. I choose not to use my powers."

"How delightful," said Mrs. Mandrake. "One could just stand on the diving board and have the water jump to *you*. It would save a lot of unnecessary flexing. Do you know, Rick, I am a little anxious about this resort."

"Because of the kidnapping?" asked Rick.

"Yes. Of course because of the kidnapping. Just before we left, Sid, the hotel manager, told me that they had received a ransom call from the kidnapper asking for forty thousand dollars apiece for the Quints."

"Wow," exclaimed Rick. "Forty thousand smackers. Times five."

"Wow, indeed," said Mrs. Mandrake. "If this were a hotel of quality, they would be asking for twenty times that, at least."

"Wait!" said Lily. "They called asking for a ransom?"

"If you can call that a ransom. I pay more than that to have my fridge cleaned."

Rick stopped in his tracks. "What?" he said. "Geez."

"My fridge," said Mrs. Mandrake, "is the size of a city block. I am serious about my Klondikes."

Lily wanted to hear more about the ransom. "Who was it who called? A man or a woman?"

"I haven't the faintest idea."

"When did they call?"

"No idea."

"Where did they say to leave the money?"

"Haven't the foggiest."

"They must have said something! When does someone have to give them the money by?"

"Darling moppet, hush—cease your charming prattle. Really—no idea whatsoever. Sid just mentioned it in passing."

Rick jumped in. "Did I, uh, did I overhear that you have a priceless necklace?"

"I do have a priceless necklace. Whether you were eavesdropping when I spoke of it, you would know better than me."

"Where does someone hide a necklace like that?" asked Rick, plucking at his knuckles. "You know, priceless. Really . . . priceless."

Mrs. Mandrake simply answered, "I have taken certain *precautions* to make sure the necklace is in no danger." She smiled.

"What would, eh, what would those be?" asked Rick.

"Why do you ask, Rick?"

"I just have the kind of inquisitive mind that loves to know . . . about necklaces . . . and, you know, precautions."

"Do you ever sit at home in the evenings, Rick, and ask yourself why you're alone?" asked Mrs. Mandrake. "I'll tell you. You don't really inspire confidence in a woman. I know the hearts of girls from six to sixty-six. When a man asks for floor plans of a woman's house and says things like 'Do you ever leave the secret door ajar?' a lady's thoughts, I'm afraid, turn from a milky-white steed and a merry wedding at the chapel in the woods to deadbolts and laser-operated motion detectors."

"Speaking of steeds, you heard of my steed?" interrupted Eddie Wax. "Her name was Stumpy and she was sired on the outer banks of Kansas and she was the bestest horse ever to gallop her way to victory and free pie."

Suddenly Lily froze. Then she pointed, a look of terror on her face.

Rick kept talking to Mrs. Mandrake. "How'd you, eh, make your big money?"

"My husband."

"How'd he make his big money?"

"He invented raisin pants."

"Raisin pants." Rick slapped himself in the forehead with the heel of his hand. "Raisin pants! All it takes is one brilliant idea, and you—"

"A BEAR!" yelled Eddie Wax, pointing where Lily pointed.

Indeed, there in the shrubs was a bear— fangs glinting, eyes yellow—ready to tear them to pieces.

Monotone!

Jasper and the Manley Boys had been wandering up the slope for an— Oh, are you interested in the bear?

All right. Okay. You win. We can do that.

Four humans cowered before the snarling bear.

"It's a grizzly," whispered Lily.

"Happily," said Mrs. Mandrake, "the soft parts of my neck are completely protected by pearls. Always remember, little girl, that it pays to pamper your jugular." She whooped defiantly, "Slash away, Bruno! There are two inches of flawless South Sea nacre between you and my lifeblood!"

Rick had gotten down on the ground and

rolled himself into a ball. He was trying to roll away but found himself lumpy.

Meanwhile, Lily tried to remember whether you were supposed to run at a bear making loud sounds. That might be what you do for a jackal. She *definitely* thought you were supposed to run at jackals. At the moment she couldn't keep anything straight. Wilderness advice kept pouring into her panicked brain. Deer are frightened off by soap. Tarantulas can jump. And bears . . . bears . . .

Suddenly she remembered. She said carefully, "Whatever you do, don't—look—in—its—eyes. And don't—turn—your—back—on it, or it will think you're prey. And speak—slowly—in a monotone—kind—of—voice."

"*Speak in a monotone?!?*" exclaimed Rick, his head between his knees.

"Goodness gracious, child, we're doomed," said Mrs. Mandrake, fanning herself. "My speaking voice is relentlessly fascinating."

With all this noise, Lily was sure the bear was going to pounce. She tensed herself.

The bear glared.

She took a step back.

The bear, however, didn't move an inch.

Lily squinted. Mrs. Mandrake had closed her eyes and held her arms out in front of her.

Lily took a step closer to the bear.

Nothing happened.

She walked right up to the bear. She reached out and touched it. "Hey," she said, "this is a stuffed bear's head."

Mrs. Mandrake opened her eyes. "How brave of you," she said.

Lily said shyly, "I was prepared for this kind of thing by my best friend's parents."

"Lily, run!" cried Eddie. "It still has its teeth!"

"It's just a head," said Lily. "It's mounted on a board."

"That means you can't shoot it through the heart!" screamed Eddie. "It's immortal!"

Everyone else looked at Eddie like he was loopy.

Meanwhile, Lily reached up and dislodged

the mounted bear's head from the branches. She examined it closely.

"That's weird," she said. "I wonder what it's doing out here?"

It was the head of a real bear that had been hunted long ago. The jaws were open in a snarl. There was a little silver plaque below the head that had the name of the hunter who had shot it, Jarris Tuttle, and the year, 1923.

Eddie was standing right next to Lily, smelling like peanut butter and whispering, "Shouldn't we leave it there?"

Lily said, "It belongs to the hotel."

"I reckon," said Eddie, "it belongs to the bear."

Something about this thought struck Lily. Slowly, she put the head down in the leaves.

"That was very startling," said Mrs. Mandrake.

"Sure was," said Rick.

Mrs. Mandrake frowned. "I didn't see much evidence of your ability to control things with your mind."

"I told you!" said Rick. "I choose not to use my powers, because it would upset the balance of"—he shrugged—"good and evil. And left and right."

"Let's keep going," said Lily. "The Quints are still out there."

They continued down the path.

Sagging in the dried leaves, the bear's head seemed to watch them as they went, peering through the shadows of the forest with its dusty glass eyes.

THE CAVE

Jasper and the Manley Boys had been wandering up the slope for an hour or so without finding anything.

It was not much fun to be in a search party with the Manley Boys. First of all, Jasper was allergic to the mountain laurel, so his nose was running. Second, the Manley Boys wanted a lot of attention for their powers of detection.

"Look!" exclaimed Jank, pointing. "That shrub is caught up a tree! We got to save it immediately!"

Jasper said, "I believe that's ivy."

"Here, boy! Here, Ivy!" said Fud, clapping smartly in a way that must have once attracted his schnauzer.

"I don't think the ivy wants to come down," said Jasper. "It is a plant."

"What do you even *know*?" said Jank, angrily. "Why are you so big faced?"

Fud said, "You're stupid."

"Jasper has goop-nose," said Fud. "Like a little baby."

Jank said, "Jasper is a little baby."

"My nose is running," said Jasper, "because I suffer from hay fever brought on by the mountain laurel."

"You eat diapers," said Jank.

"Might we continue?" said Jasper. "The Quints could be in peril."

"You're dumb," said Fud. "And your father was a sound from outer space."

"He was not a *sound*," said Jasper. "He was a signal."

"Same thing."

"It is not the same thing."

"I call that every snot-nosed person whose father was a signal from outer space gets punched," said Jank. Both he and Fud hit Jasper in the arm.

Then they kept walking.

Jasper rubbed his arms and frowned. He followed the Manleys through a little grove of birch trees. They were far up the side of the mountain.

"It would be keen if we could find the Hooper Quints first before anyone else," said Fud. "It would be yet another case solved by those daring Manley Boys."

"Righto," said Jank. "Those handsome, daring Manley Boys do it again."

"We'd like, in thanks, some free Jell-O. And we'd like to thank all of the people of this town who made our detection possible."

"You haven't solved anything yet," said Jasper.

"We solved the mystery of where that weird smell came from. From you."

Jasper was usually not a very violent person at all, but he felt violent right then. The combination of meanness and stupidity made him want to bust people up. Or cry with frustration.

For one thing, he couldn't believe the Manleys were making fun of his father for being a highly concentrated beam of information from the Horsehead Nebula.

Jasper had always taken it for granted that kindness, respect, and cooperation were logical. Nothing else was logical. Cruelty wasn't logical. Crime wasn't logical. Jasper never ceased to believe that, sooner or later, people would come to their senses and work together for the perfection of absolutely everything. There would be rings of light around towers, and boys and girls would slip through the air in antigravity halters to buffets floating over the seas, where they would eat the succulent fruits of the Venusian jungles and share giant deviled-egg sandwiches made from the huge plasma-jays of Io.

There would be a lightness over all of Earth.

Weightlessness, after all, is not just antigravity; it is learning to long for the sky more than the safety of the dirt.

"By dame is Jadper Dapp," said Jank, holding his nose. "I ab a ruddy-dose baby."

"I suffer from hay fever," began Jasper, "brought on by mountain laur—" but Fud flung out his arms and stopped them.

"Whoa," Fud exclaimed. "What's that?"

They looked up.

Fud said, "See? It's a moose—stuck in that tree!"

"Poor thing," said Jank. "Here, moose. Here, moosey!"

"I'm not sure you should worry," said Jasper. "I believe that is a stuffed moose head."

"It's trapped! It can't get down!"

"It is not trapped," said Jasper. "It is stuffed."

"I don't see it, you know, shimmying down a branch," said Fud. "Do you, Mr. Booger-nose? So I guess that's called trapped."

Jasper put his fists in his pockets. He tried to remind himself that the Manley Boys, for once, were being compassionate. They were truly worried about the stuffed moose head, and this was at least some sign of kindness.

He let them, therefore, clamber up the tree. He let them bring the moose head down and give it water, and pet it, and ask it where its mommy and legs were. He watched patiently as they became convinced that the moose head was being a jerk because it wouldn't say anything, and they started to tease it.

"You have a big nose, and it's the biggest, and it's even a snottier nose than Jasper's."

This all could have gone on for some time, but Jasper reminded them that they wanted to be the first to find the Quints.

"We would have, too, if it hadn't been for that stupid moose," said Jank.

"Yeah," said Fud. "Stupid."

"Moose," said Jank, shaking his head.

They left the moose head at the bottom of the tree and kept on walking.

They climbed higher up the mountain. They went through rocky outcroppings. They wandered through little fir woods that clustered around streams. They crawled over granite faces.

The Manley Boys were good at climbing—swift and agile.

They were walking along the base of a cliff when suddenly Jasper noticed footprints in the mud of the path. The footprints headed into the bushes. He stepped off the path.

"Hey, chaps," he hissed.

They turned around.

He pointed to the footprints.

The Manley Boys nodded. The three of them crept carefully into the bushes.

There, at the bottom of the cliff, was a cave half covered with broken tree limbs.

"That's the ticket," muttered Jank enthusiastically. He asked Fud, "You have the flashlight?" He held out his hand, peering into the darkness of the grotto.

"Sure do," said Fud. He drew it out of his belt and fiddled with it. He smacked it against his hand. "Darn. Out of batteries," he said.

Jasper cleared his throat. "That is the pepper grinder from the hotel restaurant," he said.

They looked at it, startled.

"Weird," said Jank.

"Shoot," said Fud.

"I have a flashlight," said Jasper, reaching into his pocket and pulling out a thin cylinder that he switched on.

Together, they stepped carefully into the cave.

And something was flung at them—

Jasper crouched—Fud and Jank tumbled backward—and all around them—*wings!*

"Bats!" said Jasper through the hurtling bodies. "We startled them!"

A stream of bats flew out of the cave and swooped around the woods, their wings shuffling in the air.

Jank and Fud got back to their feet. They both were saying *"Ewww,"* and brushing themselves off. "Bat spit," one said.

Jasper said, "Don't be alarmed. Bats are almost entirely harmless."

"They're gross!" said Fud. "They've touched caves."

Jasper looked at Fud for a long silent minute, then urged, "Let's go." Shining his light in front of him, he walked into the darkened entrance. Jank and Fud looked over his shoulders.

Someone had piled rocks near the entrance to make a rough staircase. The three boys went down five steps and found themselves in a big cavern.

Jasper shone the light around, illuminating a few rough furnishings: an old rug, a chair, a desk with a shortwave radio, which, though thankfully off, was tuned to an easy listening station.

There, in the corner, were five little suitcases.

The boys ran over to the suitcases and popped them open.

Inside each one, beyond a few pairs of clean underwear and a toothbrush, was a little sailor suit—and a pair of linoleum lederhosen.

"Jupiter's moons!" exclaimed Jasper. "These must belong to the Quints!" He shone the flashlight around wildly. There was a hole in the wall leading into another cavern.

Fud headed over to check it out. He handed Jasper the pepper grinder. "You hold the other light, too," he said.

Jank, looking at the passageway, guessed, "That must be where the smugglers have their boat."

Jasper said, "What smugglers?"

"The smugglers we're looking for."

"We're looking for a kidnapper."

"That must be where he keeps his boat."

Fud explained, "They always keep a boat at the river in their cave."

"I don't think it is likely there will be a river on a mountaintop."

"There's always a river."

"What use would a boat be on a mountain?"

"Well," said Fud, "at least my dad isn't a smell from outer space."

"What does that," said Jasper, "have to do with anything?"

"I'm just saying, at least my dad isn't a Martian smell."

"He was not a smell!" exclaimed Jasper, finally at the end of his rope. *"I have told you before, he was a highly concentrated beam of binary information projected from the region of the Horsehead Nebula!"*

"Sorry, you snot-nosed—"

"I am allergic to mountain laurel!"

"Hey," said Fud, "what's a neb—"

"A mysterious cloud of floating particles and gases!"

"And what's binary infor—"

"It is information made up entirely of ones and zeros!"

"Made up of ones and zeros?"

"That's what it is!"

"Heh," Jank said. "Too bad his son only inherited the zeros."

There was a moment of awed silence. Then Fud burst out, "WHOA! WHOA! WE HAVE SOLVED THE MYSTERY OF THE FUNNIEST GUY ON THE PLANET EARTH! AND IT IS MY BROTHER JANK!"

Jank repeated, "Too bad his son only inherited

the zeros, yeah? I said, 'Too bad his son only got the zeros.' "

Fud slapped his brother on the back. The two of them were laughing hysterically.

"Would you people keep it down?" said a man in a mask with a gun.

"Did you hear what he said?" screamed Fud. "This guy is the funniest guy ever! Did you hear him?"

"First, Jasper said—Jasper Dash—he said, 'The information of my dad is made up of only the ones and zeros,' and I said, 'It's too bad that—' "

"Hey! *Shh! Shhhhh!* Shut up!" the man in the black ski mask demanded. "I can hardly call this a 'secret hideout' with you making all that noise laughing like hyenas."

"Just listen," said Jank.

"Jank?" said Fud.

"Yes, Fud?" said Jank.

"There's a man with a gun."

"So there is," said the man with the gun. "About to tie you up."

"Before you gag us," said Jank, "let me tell you my joke."

"No," said the man with the gun. "I'd like to gag you first."

Jasper demanded, "Where are the Quints, you devil?"

"You're about to find out," said the man. "First I'm going to have you tie each other up." He waved the gun. "Go over there and pick up that rope." Fud picked it up. "Now wrap it tightly around Mr. Dash's ankles. Tightly! Tighter!" He waited. "Now tie a knot."

Fud hesitated. "Okay," he said.

"Tie it!"

Fud asked, somewhat embarrassed, "Can you do the shoe-tie rhyme? You know, 'Cross the river, under the bridge, bunny hops around the—'"

"Do I have to do this myself?" yelled the kidnapper.

At that point Jasper turned off his light. They were plunged into darkness.

The Manley Boys ran for the exit; Jasper,

half tied, wildly hopped. They could hear the kidnapper right near them.

Jank, tripping over the rug, fell. Jasper stopped hopping to help him up. Jank was on his knees. The man barreled toward them. Jank grabbed Jasper's head and shoved. Jasper went ricocheting into their masked opponent.

"Sorry!" said Jank and Fud, scrambling up the steps. "Don't worry—we'll be back!"

"Those brave Manley Boys have solved it again! They know," said the fleeing boy detectives, "exactly where the kidnapper's cave is . . ."

Jasper tried to pull away, but there was a tight grip of gloved fingers on his arm. He kicked and thrashed.

To no avail.

"Stop struggling, Dash," said the kidnapper. "You're not going anywhere."

And, indeed, he was not.

His ankles were tied.

Jasper Dash was trapped.

Sun and Sanding

Meanwhile, Katie had an encounter with the Cutesy Dell Twins. She was sunning herself by the pool, reading *Snazzy,* when the two of them walked out in their bathing suits and asked her about one of the articles on foot binding.

"It's a really good issue," said Katie. She didn't want to say too much. She was afraid that at any moment the Cutesy niceness could be retracted.

"Do you think this swimsuit makes me look Venezuelan?" asked one of the Twins, turning sideways. "I think that might be one of its powers."

"You look totally Venezuelan," said the other Twin. "Doesn't she?"

"Are these chairs taken?" asked the first Twin. Katie said no, and the girls sat on either side of her.

Children played in the water. They floated on inflatable wildlife, and the water around them reflected the pines.

The three girls sat in a line, their eyes blanked out by silver sunglasses.

"What a great resort," said one of the Twins.

"We're really happy we came," said the other one.

"Did you get the coupon for the free dinner?" asked the first one.

"Yeah," said Katie. "Well, Jasper did."

The Cutesy Dell Twins looked at each other over her and mouthed, *"Jasper."*

One of them said, "We think Jasper is SO cute."

The other said, "But we hope the dinner isn't a buffet."

"We hate buffets," explained the first one.

"The red light over the roast beef is creepy," said her sister.

"And the beans are super creepy."

"And potatoes au gratin make me feel like somebody wants something out of me, and they just won't ask."

Katie didn't completely understand. She ventured, "Potatoes shouldn't make anyone feel that way."

"You're right! I hate them for that!"

"So no buffet," a Twin said.

"You don't have to worry about it," Katie pointed out. "The dinner coupons were fake, anyway."

"Fake, like not from the hotel?"

"Yeah," said Katie. "Someone sent out fake coupons."

"Weird," one of the Twins said, rolling her eyes.

"That is *so* weird," said the other one.

"Who would do that?" asked the first.

Katie shrugged her shoulders. "I don't know."

"I thought you were the big mystery solver," said one of the Twins. "Like with ghosts and electrical beings."

"I've given it up," said Katie. "I'm tired of Horror Hollow. I'm totally tired of being chased and being hunted and picking up sticks to fight things off."

"It's kind of cool, though," said one of the Twins. "It makes you kind of exciting."

Katie liked the idea of being exciting.

"Well, anyway," she said, "I'm giving it up because I'm on vacation."

"Yay for vacation!" said one of the Twins.

Katie smiled. "Hey," she said, "should we get all dressed up for dinner?"

"Sure," said one of the Twins. "We could do that."

And they all were glad that she had said "We."

An hour later the three of them floated in the water on inflatable cushions. They floated in a triangle, looking up at the clouds. The pool beneath them was as blue as the sky above. They were discussing products.

"Gert is better than Clow."

"No way," said one of the Twins. "Clow is better than Gert. It's almost brave."

"Gert gets all brittle," said Katie. "I had a box once."

"Clow gets under my nails," said one of the Twins, "and people think I'm a caveman from the jungle era."

"Gert is a sweet buy."

"Clow, it's supposed to be made from really good things."

"My sister," said one of the Twins, "knows quality when she sees it."

"I just appreciate, you know, the finer things in life."

"Like she does woodworking. All the time."

"It kind of drives you crazy, doesn't it?"

"Only the hammering, because it sounds like you're inside my abdomen."

"I make tables and bureaus and things."

"They're really cool, even if they're kind of loud."

"I get a migraine headache for days if my sanding comes out sloppy. I have to stay in the dark and drink ginger ale and pretend I'm mahogany."

"I take her ice-cream floats like our grandma used to make."

Katie liked that they had hobbies. It made her feel kind of relieved. She had always thought they just worried about boys and their skin. Instead, here they were telling her about this weird little world of interests that no one even knew about. She was starting to like the Cutesy Dell Twins more and more.

And more and more, as they talked and told secrets, the overheard theft, the search parties, and the kidnapping seemed to Katie to be twelve or fifteen miles away.

Hard Times, Easy Listening

Meanwhile, Jasper Dash, Boy Technonaut, was trussed to a chair and gagged with duct tape. He couldn't even have screamed for help if he had wanted, the tape was so tight on his mouth.

He hadn't learned much about his assailant since he had been trussed. They had not talked a lot. As the mysterious kidnapper tied Jasper up, the man had murmured, "Let me just tie the loose end to the . . . that thing . . . on the back of the chair."

Jasper made muffled noises like he was trying to speak. The kidnapper yanked off the duct tape partway.

Jasper gasped. "I believe, sir, it is called a splat."

"Yeah. Thanks," said the kidnapper, slapping the tape back over the boy's mouth. "One more peep out of you and that's not going to be the only *splat* around here."

When he was done tying Jasper to the chair, the kidnapper went over to the desk and turned on the radio to the easy listening station. Out came an orchestral version of "Plaid Ballad for Stacey."

The man picked up a flashlight, turned it on, and crawled through the opening into the next cavern.

Jasper heard the man's voice echoing over the music—the kidnapper was yelling, "Would you be quiet? *BE QUIET!* I'll take off your tape, now BE QUIET."

And then Jasper heard the Quints start calling for help. They piped, "Help! Help!" while over them, the man growled, "Shut up! I told you to shut up! And for pete's sake, don't sing!"

Jasper struggled in his chair—every muscle in his civic-minded body wishing to leap up, to spring down the corridor, to biff the cad, to knock him down, to throw off the Quints' ropes and run with them to freedom.

But freedom, alas, was far away. As Jasper listened in consternation to the screams of distress, he felt a creeping little feeling. It was inside his nose. His hay fever. It was getting worse.

He sneezed. He couldn't open his mouth, of course, so the sneeze was trapped.

His nose was dripping.

He was momentarily distracted from the Quints—for he had realized something horrifying: Due to his allergy to mountain laurel, his nose was going to slowly fill up over the next hour or so. And when it did fill up, if the tape had not been ripped from his mouth, he would suffocate. And die.

One by one, the Quints' voices fell silent.

The man must be putting the tape back over their mouths, too.

Jasper decided he would explain the situation regarding his unfortunate allergic condition to the kidnapper, and they would agree manfully that if the kidnapper removed the duct tape, Jasper would be honor-bound not to speak or yell for help until he had been tagged by someone from his own team.

The kidnapper came striding out of the Quints' prison.

Jasper made mooing noises to attract his attention. He hopped the chair up and down.

The man ignored him. He lit a lamp. In its light Jasper saw the man reach into his black bag and pull out a necklace of some kind. The man looked around for some place to put it and finally hung it on the antenna of the radio.

Jasper made another attempt to explain his scheme for a reasonable agreement. Of course, all that came out were moans and a little bit more hopping.

"I just told you to shut up," growled the man.

Technically, Jasper wished to point out, the kidnapper had just told the Quints to shut up, not him; but that correction, like his idea for the gentleman's agreement vis-à-vis his hay fever, came out sounding like Jasper was barfing into a sauceboat.

The kidnapper prepared to leave the cave.

Jasper was desperate to catch his attention. He bellowed silently. His nose dribbled.

The kidnapper paused at the top of the crude stone stairs. Pensively, he looked down at his black pants. "Clothes always look better on mannequins," he said. Then he turned and walked away.

Jasper's gulps and gargles went unnoticed.

The kidnapper was gone.

For a while Jasper sat there, his head hung low.

He was, however, a boy of pluck and spirit, always ready to take on any challenge that perfidy might box and hand-deliver.

He reminded himself of that.*

He looked up.

---

*It said so in Jasper Dash #14: *Jasper Dash and His Sonic Lava Submersible.*

Aha. His ankles had been tied only very loosely by Fud, who had been unable to recall how to tie a bow. Jasper could move them a little bit.

He believed he could hop to the mouth of the cave. And he thought if he really were very careful, he could then hop the chair he was tied to up the rocky steps that led out of the cave. And then—home free. From there it would just be a two- or three-day scrape down the paths, moving a few centimeters at a time, until he reached the lodge and could be unfastened.

But what about the Quints?

Quickly, he hopped his chair over to the fissure in the rock that led to their prison. The radio played soft favorites: "Bridge Over Troubled Water" and "Babe, You're a Kernel (of Wow)."

He did not think he would fit into the hole in the wall with the chair attached to him. He slammed against it. No luck.

He would have to come back for the Quints later.

Gradually, agonizingly, he scratched his way back across the floor toward the exit.

Tottering, he swayed and clonked up the rock steps, swiveling and tipping the chair with his toes. At each move, he almost toppled. Every muscle was tense. He felt his calves ache with the strain. His arms twitched, trying instinctively to balance him as he edged his way up toward the light.

Almost there . . .

He realized that the kidnapper could come back at any time.

He had reached the entrance to the cave.

His breath was heaving through his soupy nose. In and out, it punched through torrents of mucus.

But he had made it. He wobbled on the edge, half in the sunlight, half in the darkness.

For a moment he rested, his eyes closed.

Something cool wrapped itself around his ankle.

Jasper opened his eyes.

It appeared that a Kentucky mountain asp*
lived in the cave. And it was wrapping itself
around his leg.

It was very important that Jasper didn't
move . . .

. . . except that at any moment, the kidnapper would be back . . .

His eyes above the duct tape were wide with
fear. He trembled in his seat.

And then he kicked off and went rolling
down the hillside through bracken, leaving the
asp far behind.

Whenever Jasper slowed, he'd strike out again
with his heel and keep himself rolling. Heather
mauled his cheeks. Saplings swatted him in the
face. Rocks bashed at his trunk. Still the ropes
held firm.

He looked down. As the view swung
around—forward, backward, forward, backward,
forward—he saw that he was heading straight
for a precipice. A cliff!

---

*The most poisonous of the imaginary North American snakes.

Scrabbling, he tried
to stop himself. He
stuck out his elbows
as far as possible.

BAM!

He came to rest against a small birch that leaned out over the cliff.

Safe. He was still trussed up, hanging over the edge of a chasm, but now at least he was several hundred feet away from the cave, hidden in the long grasses and mountain laurel.

Mountain laurel. To which, as we know, he was seriously allergic.

The sun shone above. The hills all around were dazzling. The air itself was golden with spores.

Jasper sputtered behind the tape. He needed to breathe. Otherwise, he would pass out soon. He sucked in as much air as possible.

The air, of course, was poison to him.

His sinuses pounded like a blacksmith forging manacles.

And suddenly he felt something slithering on his back.

The snake. It had not become fully disentangled.

And now it was sunning itself on his back.

That would be no problem, Jasper thought to himself, if he had all the time in the world. He had been suspended above enough pits of asps by arch-villains over the years to know that, come night, this one would slither back to its lair.

And under normal circumstances, remaining absolutely still for several hours would be no problem for Jasper Dash, Boy Technonaut; he had spent many months studying meditation and martial arts at an ancient monastery hidden high in some jagged mountains somewhere, and knew well how to achieve an inner calm and stillness in the most disastrous circumstances.

But within another thirty or forty minutes, Jasper would be in the convulsions of allergic suffocation—unable to breathe through mouth or nose.

And at that point, roused by Jasper's struggles, the mountain asp would wake up and get nasty.

Blinking back tears, Jasper tried to remain perfectly still.

The snake slept on his ribs.

And slowly, the tide rolled in inside his skull—dripping inexorably—and he faced the very real possibility that he, Jasper Dash, Boy Technonaut, would soon drown in his own snot.

Spurned

Lily, Eddie Wax, Mrs. Mandrake, and Rick did not have much luck. Besides the mounted bear head, they found nothing. They came back to the hotel tired and frustrated.

Mrs. Mandrake immediately stopped at the front desk and asked for the number of the fancy Schuyler-Brugghensnock Hotel in New York City so she could call them and ask what the smallest ransom demand they had ever received was. "I don't know what class of yegg you foster around here," she said, "but I have a suspicion this criminal is decidedly of the Kmart holdup variety. I absolutely refuse to be menaced by anyone who would steal from a store that sells snack cakes in bulk."

Lily wanted to go up to her room to check

to see if Katie was there, but she realized she couldn't, since it was inside someone else's bathroom. She wouldn't have minded sitting down and resting for a minute without someone talking to her. When too many people talked to her, she felt sunken and then, later, itchy.

It would be good to see Katie, though. Maybe she would be in a better mood by now. Maybe they could try to find out about the ransom call that was made to the front desk.

Lily went up and stood near the door of 46B, the room where their vacation capsule had landed. She stood there, too timid to knock. She didn't want to bother anyone. The man could be sleeping.

The lights in the hallway hummed.

She put her hands in her pockets, blew back her bangs from her eyes, and stared at the number plaque on the door.

No one came out or went in. She realized she couldn't stand there forever.

She walked around to a porch and looked out the back of the hotel.

There was Katie down below, floating in the pool with some other kids.

Lily ran for the elevators.

No sooner had she stepped out into the lobby and had time to notice that three of the animal heads on the wall were now missing than she heard a bloodcurdling scream. She stopped cold.

It was a man in a black cloak and black glasses walking out of the hotel bar. He smiled pleasantly and tipped his hat.

But then there was another scream.

This one was a voice she recognized: Mrs. Mandrake.

"I've been robbed!" shrieked Mrs. Mandrake, coming down the stairs. "The priceless Mandrake Necklace is gone!"

Lily ran over to her. "When?" asked Lily. "When did you last see it?"

"Earlier!" said Mrs. Mandrake, covering her eyes.

"Figures," said Sid, the hotel manager, nodding grimly.

Lily sprinted for the pool. There was no time to lose—she and Katie had to get on the trail of the thief!

Katie and the Cutesy Dell Twins were laughing and talking with a team of brawny water polo players.

"You could play around us," said one of the Twins. "We'll just drift."

"We can be like sand traps in golf," said the other Twin.

"Water hazards," said Katie, smiling.

Lily ran right up to the edge, her old ripped sneakers squeaking on the tiles.

"Katie!" she said. "Someone stole a priceless necklace!"

All the kids stopped talking and turned to look at her.

She backed away. Katie looked furious.

"Oh, hi, Lily," said Katie, sounding nicer than she looked. "We were just playing water polo."

"Getting in the way of people playing water

polo, more like it!" said one of the boys, and they all laughed and shouted, "Huzzah!"

"Oh . . . ," said Lily. "There's a—you know—there's a mystery . . . With the kidnapping and . . . I thought maybe you'd want to come with me. Sometime this afternoon, not now."

Katie smiled. "Sure, Lily. Maybe later." She looked around at her new friends and then asked Lily, without much force, "Maybe you want to come swimming?"

"No," said Lily, her hair falling over her eyes.

Everyone waited awkwardly for a minute. Some of the water polo guys treaded water.

Lily didn't want to take up too much of Katie's time, since Katie looked busy on the inflatable cushion, so she asked, "Have you, um, seen Jasper?"

"No," said Katie. "He's probably goofing off somewhere."

"Okay," said Lily. "See you later. I'll be . . .

whenever you're done . . . I'll be in our room."
She corrected herself, "Not in. I guess we can't
go in. I'll be outside our room in the hallway.
Waiting. Okay?"

Suddenly one of the water polo boys
shouted, "Victory goes to the sharkiest!" and
they all raised their brown arms and barked like
sea dogs.

Lily turned and walked quickly back inside
the hotel.

She didn't want to be stared at like that any
longer than was absolutely necessary.

Behind her, Katie floated on her raft, watching Lily go. Katie already knew that a priceless
necklace had been stolen, of course; she had
heard the thief at work. She wanted to tell Lily
her clues, but doing that would mean she would
probably end up having to help find the burglar,
and that was the last thing Katie wanted to do at
that moment.

She felt a little sick and empty, though,
watching Lily retreat. Even as she turned her

head and put on a quick smile for the Cutesy Dell Twins, Katie was anxiously planning for dinner, when, she promised herself, she would make it all up to Lily. Once Jasper got back, she would include him and Lily in the little dinner party with the Twins. They would dress up for the restaurant and sit there like grown-ups around a table, and Lily wouldn't embarrass her.

Katie vowed to herself that Lily would have a good time, and would like the Twins, and would forgive her for what had just happened. Then Katie would tell Lily and Jasper about what she'd heard that afternoon—the burglar's bungling—and Jasper and Lily would have all sorts of startling ideas about things like *motive, opportunity,* and *means.* They would argue about who could be the guilty party while Jasper balanced the forks and knives on top of each other, which he always did absentmindedly when he was excited by the conversation. The Twins would watch the three of them talk it all through and would be impressed that Katie and her friends were so used to adventure. And everything would be fine again.

Katie promised herself this as she floated on her raft with the noise of water polo sloshing around her. The boys crowed. The Twins squealed. The ball slapped the water. Katie floated like an island, touching no one, suspended in blue.

THE MIND-BOGGLING ACTION OF IMMUNOGLOBULIN E

And what, meanwhile, was happening with Jasper?

Not much, *in a sense*—because he was tied to a chair and couldn't move. But, my friends, let's look a little closer.

There—at the microscopic level—in Jasper Dash's pure and noble bloodstream—now clogged with histamines and immunoglobulin E*—down at the level where antibodies sounded the alarm at the invasion of foreign microbes— there, we see the action unfolding like the most furious aeroplane dogfight you've ever seen in a

---

*Are you trying to tell me that a paragraph that uses phrases like "histamines and immunoglobulin E" might not be very, um, *interesting*?

World War II newsreel: machine guns rattling, riddling wings with bullets—wings tipping toward the earth—tumbling—torn engines spewing smoke into the sky! Parachutists bailing! Yes, indeed!

SEE the allergen enter the blood!

THRILL as Jasper's hypersensitive plasma cells secrete *immunoglobulin E!*

SHRIEK WITH TERROR as squadrons of immunoglobulin E molecules mob Jasper's dizzy mast cells—*provoking the release of bloating histamines!*

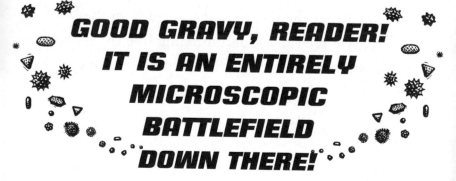

GOOD GRAVY, READER! IT IS AN ENTIRELY MICROSCOPIC BATTLEFIELD DOWN THERE!

I would like to take a moment to point out to those Hollywood actionmongers in their double-breasted suits and their hip, sticky-uppy hair-dos—those Sunset Boulevard "dream weavers" with their endless car chases, relentless gunplay, Ninja kicks, shattering windows, bombings, bazookas, back-alley fisticuffs, flipping cop cars, and sultry ballads to the helicopter—I would like to point out to *you*, sirs, that here we have a scene of incredible suspense and terror (I, for one, have not been able to go to the bathroom for the two days it has taken me to write this page) that consists *entirely of some guy lying absolutely still in a pretty mountain pasture for seven hours.*

What do you say to *that*, my Tinseltown friends?

Hm?

PIP PIP, LADS! *IS YOUR DAY DREARY?*

That's why you need to scramble down to the post office, ring the service bell with a flat and courteous hand, and—fast as lightning—send away for your

Jasper Dash

AGGRAVATED HAY-FEVER PLAY SET

WITH ANTIBODY ACTION FIGURES!

• *Bloodstream play mat sold separately* •

Bobby Plasma!

Immunoglobulin E!

Killer T cell!

Antigen Sam!
(with shortwave radio)

The Histamine Sisters!

Each action figure available for 3 proof-of-purchase seals from any jar of Chocolate, Mint, Banana, or new Cheddar-Flavored GARGLETINE Breakfast Drink!

How does JASPER DASH, Boy Technonaut, keep his blood so fearless, so brave, so ready to defend against any and all potential threats—even cat dander? By drinking a healthy glass of GARGLETINE each morning as the dawn chorus begins to sing on the electrical wires!

*"Want to keep your blood real clean?
Daily, guzzle Gargletine!"*

Gargletine

BREAKFAST DRINK

Meanwhile, in the Nostrils

But, um, of course, that really isn't what Jasper himself was thinking about.

Jasper himself was not excited about his entertainment potential.

He was, instead, lying, head upside down, on the edge of a cliff, trying not to twitch. From the northern dome of his skull, the slow ice age had begun to creep in earnest. The mucus had begun to harden in ridges and clots. He could feel the snot form stalactites and stalagmites, blocking passages while his tiny breaths wandered like lost spelunkers through nasal caverns. His every breath clambered and squelched through his nostrils.

Finally, he started gagging. One nostril was entirely clogged. Corked. Only a tiny crack admitted air to the other nostril. He could hardly breathe. He was beginning to panic.

Jasper turned his head gradually . . . gradually . . .

He pressed his nose against the granite, shutting his one free nostril.

With all passages blocked, he tried desperately to blow the clog out of his other nostril.

The snake, happily dreaming of ancient religions where snakes were hand-fed hard-boiled eggs by nuns in chain mail, sighed, licked its thin lips, and shifted in the warm sun on Jasper's back.

Trembling, Jasper forced air behind the plug. He closed his eyes. Veins stood out on his forehead.

Nothing. The snot would not budge.

He relaxed. He opened his eyes.

His breath whined—a tiny trickle—through the one remaining nostril.

Upside down, he looked across the chasm he lay next to. On the other side of it, there was a meadow full of Queen Anne's lace.

He was not allergic in the slightest to Queen Anne's lace.

So Jasper Dash, Boy Technonaut, lay there staring longingly at the Queen Anne's lace, and thinking how sweet life would be, how perfect in almost every detail, if he could only be bound and gagged with a deadly snake sleeping on him over in *that* meadow.

That, he thought, would make him the happiest boy alive.

Which goes to show you that everything is relative.

KATIE EATS CROW,
OR,
THE BUFFET OF SORROWS

"I cannot imagine being anywhere worse than this buffet," said one of the Cutesy Dell Twins to Katie.

"No way," Katie agreed.

"Maybe being stuck in some stupid cave," said the other Twin, who then shivered, momentarily bewildered by a stray image in her brain that was actually from a previous life two thousand years before, in which she and her sister had been priestesses and had had to dress in weird metal clothes and hand-feed eggs to serpents.

Katie, the Cutesy Dell Twins, and Lily sat at a table in the grand dining hall of the hotel. Around them, men were dressed in black bow ties and starched collars, and women wore glittering dresses. Some ladies wore peacock feathers in their head scarves. There was talking and champagne. A jazz band—Dix Wickerbasket and His Amazing Dix-Chords—played old dance tunes.

Katie was anxious for several reasons. She still hadn't told Lily that she'd actually heard the theft of Mrs. Mandrake's necklace. Also, she really wanted the Cutesy Dell Twins to like Lily and Jasper. But Lily was acting very shy, and Jasper hadn't come back for dinner.

Outside the windows it was still light, even though it was eight o'clock in the evening. The sun was just starting to go down over the mountains. It glittered on the rivers and highways far, far beneath them.

"So you spent the day with Eddie Wax?" said one of the Cutesy Dell Twins to Lily.

"Yes," she said. She didn't want to say any more.

"What did you think of him?"

Katie watched Lily's face. She could tell Lily wanted to say the right thing—but that Lily also didn't want to be mean. "He was nice," said Lily, who thought again, and then admitted, "He talked about his horse a lot."

The Twins exchanged glances. "Oh yeah," they said. "Yeah."

One of them said, as if innocent, "So you think he's cute?"

"Yeah, cute?" asked the other one.

Lily froze. "He has nice . . . freckles," she said. "But he's . . . he . . . talks . . . about . . ." She stopped.

The Twins both leaned forward. "He is completely crazy," said one.

"Koo-koo loco," said the other.

Lily said, "I've actually only read one of his books. And then met him today. I don't really know him well."

One of the Twins touched her nose, as if to say, "Right on the nose." She said, "He *only has one book.*"

The other Twin explained, "He *thinks* he was

the star of a horse book series. But he wasn't. That's just what he dreamed of. In fact . . . *Stumpy Rides to Glory,* his book—it was one of those *DEAD HORSE books.*"

"You know? Like the dead dog books?"

"Or the dead deer books?"

"It was a total dead horse book."

Lily nodded. "That's what I thought I remembered. Stumpy . . . something happened to Stumpy the horse, didn't it?"

The Twins nodded. "Caught a weird horse disease saving orphans in a hailstorm," they said.

"After the book, someone had the horse stuffed and they took it around to libraries to show kids."

"On *wheels.*"

"It made the worst squeaking noise. The axles were totally amateur."

"My sister the perfectionist!"

Suddenly Rick loomed over them. He said, "Hi there, Lily! I see you found your friends."

Katie dropped her fork. The voice . . .

"One of my friends isn't back yet," said Lily.

"That's too bad," said Rick. "Hey, I had a great time today. Didn't you?"

Lily shrugged. "It was okay," she said uneasily. "I mean, we were looking for those kids who are in danger . . ."

"But it was such a great opportunity to get to know a wonderful lady like Mrs. Mandrake."

Rick's voice sounded a little bit like the assistant manager in a second-rate electronics store that specialized in phone adapters.

Katie forgot she was not supposed to be solving mysteries. In that instant, she knew just one thing: This man was the burglar. She rose from her seat and pointed at Rick. "*You* stole that necklace!" she said. "I know the sound of your voice! I'd know your voice anywhere! I heard you talking while you searched the room!"

"I think you must be mistaken, young lady," said Rick.

"I am not mistaken," she said, still pointing at him. "I heard you!"

"I was with Lily all afternoon," said the man.

"It was you!"

He laughed. "Oh, what? Maybe my 'astral self' projected out of my body through some kind of thought control?" He chuckled. "That's really not very likely, kid. Dream on. Great suggestion."

"He honestly was with me all afternoon," said Lily quietly.

"You snuck into that old woman's room when people from the search parties were coming in to go to the bathroom!"

"I didn't go near the bathrooms," said Rick.

Lily said, "He really didn't, Katie."

"I held it," said Rick, not without pride. "I waited outside."

"I know you stole that necklace," said Katie.

He nodded and reached across the table and patted her on the head. "I'm sure you think so, kid."

"*Don't be—don't— Don't you think you'll get away with it!*" Helplessly outraged at crime despite herself, Katie rose and, pointing again, announced to the whole dining room, "*THIS MAN STOLE THE MANDRAKE NECK-LACE!*"

There was silence. People looked up from their meals.

People put down their napkins.

Still silence.

Rick cleared his throat. People waited for an explanation.

He said, "I was with Lily, Mrs. Mandrake, and that horse kid."

Mrs. Mandrake said, "It is true. This gentle-man marauded me all afternoon without cease. He could not have stolen my necklace from my room while we walked together. That appears to be one of the only benefits of spending time with him."

Katie felt faint. Everyone was looking at her. Everyone was staring at their table.

The Cutesy Dell Twins were mortified. One of them said to the other, "Okay. Do you want to die first or me?"

Katie wanted to hide under the table. Lily reached out and held her friend's hand tightly.

Everyone wondered what to do at this awkward moment.

Sid, the hotel manager, standing at the back of the dining room, called nervously, *"MUSIC! MUSIC! HOW ABOUT MORE MUSIC?"*

The diners looked around, startled. Someone in the band picked up a trombone. Everyone clapped as the band began playing and a singer swept out onstage in a beautiful silk gown, a marcel wave in her hair, and grasped the microphone.

Rick smiled at Katie and walked off.

"I know I heard him," said Katie.

"Or someone who sounded like him," said one of the Twins sharply.

"Okay, I'm going under the table now," said

the other Twin, "and I'm only coming up when there's more normalness to breathe."

Lily still held Katie's hand. "I believe you," she said. Katie blinked back tears, looking at her old friend, faithful even now.

In between blinks, she saw the Twins disappear.

Katie said, "I swore I wasn't going to solve any mysteries this weekend."

"Don't worry," said Lily, determined. "We'll figure it out."

"I don't want to figure it out." Katie's voice was high and wiry, and filled with tears. "I dressed up specially for tonight."

"You look really nice," said Lily.

"Thanks," said Katie, but she didn't really mean it, because she didn't feel very pretty right then.

"Katie," urged Lily, and she didn't need to say anything else.

Katie wiped at her eyes.

At a nearby table, Rick stretched himself

and lit a cigar. The Dix-Chords blared the introduction to some song.

Outside, the sun was going down, and Katie and Lily sat miserably alone at their table while the Cutesy Dell Twins crawled toward the water polo team's feed trough. The setting sun cast great corridors of light through the mountains and the windows, and the brass flashed up onstage, and the beautiful singer began, to the tinkling of the piano:

"*They say the earth has oxygen*
Enough for twenty billion men
And for their twenty billion gals
And assorted pets and pals.

"*But, dear, though there is always air—*
Whenever you are standing there
About to close me in your grasp
All I do is swoon and gasp . . .
Because . . .

"*I'm brrrreathless whenever you're near . . .*"

The band picked up the pace. People got up to dance. Katie heard a hideous high-pitched shrieking noise and looked over. Dr. Schmeltzer was dancing with Mrs. Mandrake. He screamed the whole time to echolocate other couples. His mouth was big and oval and ugly, but he actually was pretty good at the fox-trot.

"My knees get weak
My elbows creak
I tremble as in fear.
I get all shy
Though you're my guy
I'm breathless whenever you're near."

People, unsettled by Katie's accusation, still stared over at their table.

"I wish Jasper were here," muttered Katie.

8:17

Breathless, Jasper lay on the mountainside, held up by a sapling, tied to a chair, choking, with a venomous snake coiled on his back.

His breathing had been whittled down almost to nothing—a tiny screeching whistle.

That high, faint whistle was all that stood between him and death.

His muscles were sore from holding himself still all day. Rocks had dug into his arms and hands. He trembled with exhaustion.

Soon, he thought, *by Jupiter . . . soon . . .*

The sun was going down over the mountains. Ten minutes more, maybe, and the snake would wake up. Ten minutes more, and it would slither home, and Jasper could start to work off the ropes, rip off the tape, and then . . . Almost with tears, he thought of the glory, the freedom, the splendor, of picking his nose.

He thought of this, lying prone, looking up at the ruddy sunlight falling on the mountain. Only ten more minutes.

But then, with a small *tic,* the last passage into Jasper's nostril sealed up.

Jasper Dash was entombed in his own mucus.

He struggled without moving his body. The silver tape heaved around his mouth. His head lifted and dropped.

He couldn't believe it—only a few minutes more—and now—his lungs—they felt so hideously empty . . .

8:18

"My throat gets frogged
My nose gets clogged
My eyes, they burn and tear.
I gasp for air
I claw my hair
I get brrrrreathless whenever you're near."

"Wow," said Katie. "This song really makes you want to breathe freely, doesn't it?"

"Shouldn't Jasper be back by now?" said Lily. "I hope he's okay."

8:19

Jasper couldn't help it. His body needed air.

A twitch, at first . . . his head bucking . . . the tape flexing over his clamped mouth . . .

The serpent, irritated, began to stir.

Jasper tried to hold himself still . . . but clamor was everywhere within him.

He began to thrash. The ropes held him fast.

Lashed to the chair, he bucked back and forth—the asp toppled to one side—and, groggy, hissed—Jasper helplessly beat against the ground—losing hope—losing breath—losing consciousness—the snake, angry, raised its fanged head—

Jasper—seeing stars—began to pass out—

The snake lunged at his throat.

8:20

"*I retch and drool*
My liquids pool
My pupils disappear.
My jaw just flaps
My lungs collapse
I get brrrreathless whenever you're near—

"*I gag and fall*
And voiceless call
For an ambulance to appear.
I cough and hack—
You slap my back—
But though you smack
I fade to black—
Each alveolar sac

Completely slack—
For I go BREATHLESS,
So totally BREATHLESS,
So helplessly BREATHLESS
WHEN—EVER—YOU'RE—
NEEEARRRRRRRRR!"

Everyone burst into applause.
It was a delightful evening.

ASP AT 8:20

Jasper—his senses fading—saw the serpentine head approaching his throat in slow motion—whipped his chaired body as hard as he could away—away—away.

And went tumbling off the cliff.

He was unable to scream as he fell.

KATIE EATS HUMBLE PIE

Dessert usually is fun. It was not fun that evening, however, for Katie and Lily. They felt as if everyone was still staring at them because of Katie's accusation. The Black Forest cake seemed dry. The New York cheesecake tasted more like Delaware.

While the girls forced themselves to eat dessert, they had to listen to the Cutesy Dell Twins and the water polo team across the room laugh heartily at all kinds of jokes no one else could hear. Katie had to see the Cutesy Dell Twins looking at her and whispering. They had to watch Dr. Schmeltzer get served plate after plate of mosquitoes, which he ate with gusto like popcorn shrimp.

They heard Mrs. Mandrake say in passing, "There's that little girl who made the big fuss."

"Don't listen," whispered Lily, but it was too late. Katie had heard.

After that, the two girls sat on either side of the table, not eating. Katie didn't like being called a "little girl." She felt like everyone thought she was an idiot.

"I believe that you really heard the thief," said Lily. "Even though you didn't . . ." She trailed off.

"What?" said Katie.

Lily shrugged.

"You mean I didn't say anything to you," said Katie.

"Yeah," said Lily. "I didn't know you heard anything. Until just now."

Katie looked at her friend. She wished, in a funny kind of way, that Lily would get angry with her. She wished Lily would yell at her for not saying something about the robbery earlier.

They sat there, not talking about the crime

for several minutes. This would have been a great time for them to review motive, means, and opportunity—those three essential things that a good detective has to establish about every crime. It would have been a good time for them to discuss the *motive* for kidnapping the Quints and then stealing the necklace—and whether the same person even committed both crimes, or whether the crimes weren't related. It would have been a great time to discuss who had the *opportunity* to commit each crime. It also would have been a super chance to ask who would bother to send out mysterious invitations to a free dinner which was not, in fact, free, but $21.95 a head.

Yes, it would have been a great time to do and say a lot of things. Instead, the two girls just stared at the tablecloth and listened to the rustling of the dancers' skirts and dresses.

This is what tension between friends can do: ruin a perfectly good opportunity to pursue the kidnapper of singing quintuplets.

Finally, Katie said, "So that guy Rick really didn't go to the bathroom when everyone else did?"

"No," said Lily, embarrassed she couldn't give a more positive answer. "He really didn't. But almost everyone else did. Eddie Wax did, for example."

"Eddie Wax," said Katie. "Is he here now?"

Lily looked around. She shook her head.

"What was he like?" asked Katie.

"Nice. I feel really bad about his horse. He loved that horse."

"He sounds a little insane," said Katie. She shrugged. "But freckly." She sighed and pushed away the last of her cake. "I can't eat any more. I feel like the cake is filled with eyes."

Lily squinted at her.

"Everyone is staring."

"No, they're not," said Lily.

"Yes, they are. They think I'm crazy."

"They're not thinking about it anymore."

"Yes, they are."

"There's other stuff going on," said Lily.

Katie turned her fork upside down on her plate.

"Let's go to the bathroom. I need to hide for a minute."

They got up and walked to the exit.

When they got to the bathroom, Katie sat inside a marble stall and said, "You can leave if you want to. I just need to sit here and calm down for a minute."

Lily said, "I'll just lean against the counter."

"Don't lean against the counter," said Katie. "You'll get splash-back on your sweatshirt."

"I'm not near the sink."

They rested for a minute. Other women came into the restroom, and used it, and left.

"Are you still there, Lily?" said Katie.

"Yeah."

"Why don't you leave for a minute?"

Lily hesitated, then said, "Oh. Okay."

She started to leave.

"Hey," said Katie. "Hey, Lily, are you still there?"

"Yeah. I'm near the door."

"I'm really sorry. I was kind of a jerk earlier today."

Lily shrugged. "Um, that's okay."

"Okay?"

"I'm fine," said Lily. "You weren't . . . Well, you weren't too much of a jerk."

Katie thought about this, then laughed a little. "Like, only eight out of ten?"

"Six," said Lily, smiling. "Or six point two."

"Thanks," said Katie. "You know you're my best friend?"

Lily shuffled nervously. She didn't like people talking about that kind of thing out loud. "Sure," she said. "Hey," she added in a reassuring voice, "we're going to solve this mystery, aren't we? Together?"

"Yeah," said Katie. "Maybe."

"Don't worry," said Lily. "When Jasper gets back, we'll have a big discussion and figure out who's the guilty party."

Katie sat for a minute before she said, "I feel like I'm the guilty party."

Lily stood awkwardly with her hand on the door. Finally, she said, "I'll go up to the Sky Suite and meet you there when you're ready."

"All right," said Katie, from inside the stall. Her voice echoed. She heard Lily go out. She sat bent forward on the closed toilet seat, her elbows on her knees. She stared at the grain of the wood on the stall door.

Lily, meanwhile, walked across the lobby. She hoped Katie felt better. She paused for a moment and looked back toward the bathroom door. Still closed. Diners from the restaurant strolled out into the lobby to chat or to grab croquet mallets and head out to the lawn for an evening game. Lily passed by huddled groups that discussed the crimes in quiet tones.

As she was heading for the elevators, she noticed an odd shape scurrying down a hallway.

She trotted a short way along the corridor to see what it was.

It was Eddie Wax.

He was coming out of his room, carrying something bulky in a bag and looking terrified.

Lily stepped backward into one of the elevators. She let the door close in front of her, but she hit the Hold button, which kept the elevator from moving. In a minute the doors slid open again.

Carefully, she peeked out. Eddie was sneaking away.

She followed him, noting his room number. He looked very worried.

MANLEY BOYS TO THE RESCUE!

Meanwhile, Jasper was falling thirty— Oh, I'm sorry. You probably want to hear more about Katie and Lily and their winning ways. Okay, fine. We'll just leave poor Jasper hanging in the air until you're ready. I'll start over.

Meanwhile, Katie stepped out of the bathroom, feeling a bit better after sitting there alone for a while. She headed for the grand staircase.

She hadn't even made it across the lobby when the huge front doors slammed open and the Manley Boys rushed in. They stumbled on the rug. They were a mess. Their faces were scratched and twigs and leaves hung off their varsity sweaters.

"We found a—"

"Jasper Dash has been kidnapped!"

"It's a cave!"

"He's been kidnapped!"

"Jasper Dash!"

"He's—"

"Excuse me," said Sid, coming over to them. "Pardon me." He held his hands over their mouths. "If every hour on the hour," he hissed with some menace, "people are going to stagger into this lobby and make catastrophic announcements—kidnappings, thefts, secret caves, alien abductions, radiated salamanders, trolls, underground cities, mysterious and deadly games— the hotel management would be grateful if instead of shrieking about local disaster so all the other guests can hear, you could please fill out this simple, quiet complaint form, available from the concierge."*

"But Jasper, he's—," said Fud.

"Those handsome Manley Boys, they've solved another—," said Jank.

"Hup! Hup!" Sid led them over to the desk.

---

*See appendix B.

He handed them two forms. They bowed their heads and started writing. The hotel manager stopped them, grabbed their pencils, and said, "In pen, please. Press hard. This has to be in triplicate."

While Jank, who thought the alphabet was for sissies, gripped his pen and tried to tell their story in hearty, masculine pictograms, Fud said, "It took us a real long time to get back. Without Jasper."

"Not because he knew the way better or anything," said Jank, looking up from his drawings. "We just got turned around from, uh, magnetism. And lost the map climbing a tree. So it's been a while since we left him."

Katie rushed over. "Where is he?" she demanded. "Why didn't you stay with him?"

"Because we were saving him," explained Fud, "by running away. So we could tell everyone."

"Tell them *what*? That you're *chickens*?" cried Katie.

"We had to tell the people that we found the cave," said Jank. "We are the well-built sons of ace detective Bark Manley."

"Is Jasper in danger?" Katie said. "What's going on? Where?"

"In the cave!" said Fud.

"What cave?"

"We found."

"Where?"

"On the mountain."

"Where?"

Fud emphasized, "THE. CAVE."

Katie emphasized, "Where. Is. The. Cave?"

"The. Cave. Is. On. The. Mountain."

"Where. On. The. Mountain?"

"IN. THE. CAVE."

Before this moronic conversation could go on any longer, suddenly, across the lobby, there was a bloodcurdling scream.

Eddie Wax Heads for the Hills

Eddie Wax made his way down the service stairs, a grain sack filled with something lumpy in his arms.

Lily walked carefully behind him. She had learned various tricks about how to shadow people from Katie and Jasper when they talked about their previous adventures. Most of these clever techniques, though, were only good if you were following people on a crowded street. When there was no one else around, it was a different story.

By the time Lily reached the bottom of the service stairs, Eddie was gone.

She looked around. One set of doors led into the laundry room. One led into the garbage pit.

One led to a breezeway and the outdoors—and that door was still swinging slightly.

Lily opened the inner swinging door, and then, very slowly, the door to the outside.

There, in the glaring lights of the back parking lot, Eddie Wax, with his mysterious package, was making a run for the woods.

In a moment, he had disappeared into the darkness.

Time, Lily thought, *to go through that bathroom to the Sky Suite and find Jasper's lock-picking tools.*

She was going to pay a visit to Eddie Wax's room.

DR. SCHMELTZER TO THE RESCUE!

"Pardon," said Dr. Schmeltzer to the people in the lobby. "I did not mean to startle."

Everyone breathed a sigh of relief, or perhaps irritation.

"I could not help but overhear the young gentlemen," said Dr. Schmeltzer. "They appear to have been disoriented. I suspect they no longer can state with clarity where lies the grot within which their benighted playmate is immured."

No one knew what he was talking about. They nodded and prepared to do something else.

"The cave," explained the cloaked professor, "where their friend is being held. They don't know where it is."

Exasperated, Fud insisted, "The. Cave. Is. On. The. Mountain."

"But we, young man, are on the mountain, and we are not in the cave. My point, ladies and gentlemen, is this"—everyone turned to listen—"If young Jork and Flick Mandeley here had navigated not by sight, but by echolocation, as the clever bat does, they would have no trouble leading us back through the darkness to the cave. But because . . ."

Everyone groaned.

"Wait!" cried the professor. "Wait, before you dismiss me!" He swept his cape back and declared, "I, good people—I know where the cave is! Three years ago I went there to conduct a survey among the bats. Indeed, it was to return to the aforementioned cave that I came to this hotel. Thus: Using echolocation, I, ladies and gentlemen, I can conduct a search party thither posthaste."

"I'll go with you," said Katie. "Let me just find my friend Lily, and I'll be right back!"

"Very good, young lady," said Dr. Schmeltzer. "I will wait for you on that landing."

Katie ran up to their room—or to the room that led into their room—and found the door ajar and the occupant of 46B sitting in bed. "If you're looking for that girl with bangs over her eyes," he said, "she went into the bathroom. I think she's building something in there."

Katie ran to find Lily in the Sky Suite. Quickly, throwing their hands around a lot, they each explained what had happened to them since they had parted in the restroom. They agreed they'd split up: Lily would go break into Eddie Wax's room and see if she could find any clues. Katie would go with Dr. Schmeltzer to find Jasper.

"I'm glad we're working together again," said Lily.

"Me too." Katie nodded, then looked down at her good skirt. "My assignment for next time: Find some nice-looking shoes that wear really well for crime fighting."

Quickly, the two girls grinned at each other.

Then they set off running. Lily went through drawers in the crime lab, looking for Jasper's lock-picking device. Katie threw off her fancy shoes and hopped back through the bathroom of 46B, pulling on her sneakers.

The man in 46B had turned over on his side and wrapped the pillow around his head.

Katie ran downstairs. As promised, Dr. Schmeltzer was waiting on the landing, hanging from the railing, in fact, grooming himself with his teeth.

"I'm ready," said Katie.

"Good, then," he said, nipping at vermin on his cape. "Let's be off."

With a horrifying shriek, he dropped to the ground, swirled his cape, and ran for the exit.

Katie ran right behind him.

Down the Cliff

Jasper hit the ground hard. He slid. The chair cracked beneath him.

He slid on shale.

He rolled on scree.

He came to rest near a river. It chortled over stones.

The snake was gone, but Jasper was still suffocating.

His legs were free now; that wouldn't help if he passed out again.

He rolled to one side and the other, writhing.

Something was lumpy under his stomach, pressed against the rocks.

He jumped—thinking it was the snake.

But no—it was just Fud's pepper grinder, which Jasper had shoved in his belt.

If only it had been an item of some use . . . something that could . . .

But then he had an idea.

Trembling, he smeared himself along the ground. He rubbed his stomach on the stone; and as he did so, the pepper grinder turned. It left behind it a trail of freshly ground pepper.

Feverishly, Jasper shoved his nose into the spicy mix. He snorted in as hard as he could. Nothing.

He sucked in harder—but just succeeded in choking on globs of sputum like softball pitches of cottage cheese.

He buried his nose again in the peppery dirt and drew breath with all his might.

And—miraculously—Jasper Dash sneezed.

He sneezed so hard that the plugs shot out of his nose. He sneezed so hard that he kicked with his feet, and the chair cracked again beneath him and fell apart.

He lay in the dying sunlight, listening to the pittering of the river, breathing deeply, fully at last. Bubbles of goobery joy slid down his cheeks. Air, sweet air, sweet air filled with spores, flooded back into his lungs to begin the whole cycle again.

But now Jasper had time.

He kicked with his legs and broke the chair to pieces. The back and one of the struts hung awkwardly from the ropes, but the rest lay on the rocks of the little valley where he had come to rest.

Jasper put his knees up near his face. He scraped them across the frayed corners of the duct tape. He clapped them together on the edges of the tape, seizing the corners between them. He pulled.

Slowly, at first, but then more easily, he pulled the duct tape off his mouth.

It was stuck now on his knees.

He threw his head back and breathed deeply.

He leaned against a rock.

His hands were tied together, but that hardly mattered. He could walk back to the hotel. He would follow the river.

Jasper Dash, exhausted, stood up and began walking, entirely unaware of the pack of wolves that had snuck up behind him.

LILY USES HER HEAD

Lily stood before the door to Eddie Wax's room. Looking both ways along the hallway, she drew a gadget out of her pocket. It looked like a little cylinder with thin wires sticking out of one end and a toggle switch on the other.

It was Jasper Dash's Astonishing Universal Lock Pick.

She pressed it up against the keyhole. She flicked the switch.

The cylinder clicked quietly as little wires were extended. They felt the tumblers of the lock, jumped into formation, and began spinning.

In a moment the door swung open.

Lily stepped inside and closed the door behind her.

The room was dark, lit only by the glow of evening. Lily set her jaw and waited for her eyes to adjust.

Eddie had a single suitcase open on a stand. On the floor there was a saddle with all of the rest of the tack, as it's called—all the horse straps—laid out around it. He had attached the bit, which usually goes into the horse's mouth, to a lamp he'd moved to the floor. He had also attached a feed bag filled with oats to the lamp.

Lily leaned down over the saddle and picked up the bridle.

It looked very much as if Eddie Wax had been riding an imaginary horse.

It looked very much, in other words, as if Eddie Wax, truly, was insane.

A little chill went up Lily's spine.

She put down the bridle and began rummaging around in the suitcase. There were three identical pairs of blue overalls, some underwear, some socks, and his tuxedo, bow tie, and Brylcreem.

Lily straightened up and looked around the room again.

Now her attention was drawn to the bed.

In the half-light, she could see that there was a lump in it—an irregular little lump near the pillow.

She walked carefully around the bed skirts, approaching the lump.

She reached up to seize hold of the covers.

She felt danger all around her.

She pulled the cover back.

And there, grinning up at her from the bed, was a head.

A mounted weasel head.

QUIT WHILE YOU'RE
A STUFFED WEASEL'S HEAD

Lily lifted the stuffed weasel's head.

That's odd, she thought. *Eddie must be the one who hid that bear head in the woods. And took the other missing heads from the lobby. I wonder why . . .*

And with that, she froze.

Because someone had put a key in the door.

An Element of Surprise

Katie and Dr. Schmeltzer walked through the woods. Katie carried a flashlight. Dr. Schmeltzer just kept shrieking.

It was not an easy hike. The pine trees and fir trees clustered tightly around them. Everything was dark and needly. Everything brushed against them. Everything prickled and poked. Dr. Schmeltzer walked into branches and let them snap back. Katie kept her hands in front of her. Otherwise, the branches slapped across her nose.

They crossed the little bridges over mountain streams that Lily had crossed by day. Now, however, there was nothing charming about them. Beneath them, black chasms hung. Water gargled in unseen holes, past unseen spikes of rock and grim little pools and mossy banks where water rats could hide.

As they walked, Dr. Schmeltzer's shrieking voice echoed through the desolate hills, as if calling forgotten mountain ogres to join in a feast. The hugeness of the peak above weighed on Katie. She could hear the impossible heights and the terrifying drops recorded in Dr. Schmeltzer's yell.

"Um," she said, "you know, we're going out to find a cave with an armed bandit in it."

"Yes, my dear," said Dr. Schmeltzer. "Unless he's out on a foul errand."

"Yeah. My point is that maybe the element of surprise is kind of ruined by having you screaming continually at the top of your lungs."

"I am, unfortunately, unable to find the cave without it."

"But, see, when we find the cave, the kidnapper might be prepared for us. That is, if he knows an hour, an hour and a half in advance that we're on our way."

Dr. Schmeltzer frowned. "Do you want me to lead you to the cave or not?"

Katie nodded. "Yes, of course."

"So we go by the way I know."

"If there's any way—"

"The way I know is entirely using the language of our friends the bats."

"Yeah. Our friends."

Dr. Schmeltzer let out another bloodcurdling scream.

This is definitely getting old, thought Katie.

Eddie Returns

Eddie Wax huffed like a winded spaniel and shut the door behind him. He turned on the light and sat down on the bed.

"How are you, horsey?" he asked the floor and the lamp. "Were you made by a finer hand than mine to take me to all the great places on the earth?" He went over and stroked the lamp's mane, which it didn't have. He asked the lamp, "Are you going to take me to the pyramids and to Paris, France, Europe? That's," he said sternly, "what a good horse does."

Lily heard all this and did not feel any better about being in his room with him.

"Have you been watching Prell?" he asked the lamp. He went over and pulled back the covers of the bed. There was the weasel head. He said, "You're next, Prell. They ain't gonna keep you all boxed up in here like a saltine cracker. A hairy saltine cracker. Every animal should be free."

Lily was hiding inside the entertainment center, curled up on the shelf beneath the TV. She may have been in the entertainment center, but she was not entertained. She felt sorry for Eddie—but she was afraid of his lunatic ravings about stuffed animals.

"They say if you love something, set it free," said Eddie Wax. "But what if you don't love anything?"

Eddie sighed.

"Then," he said, "you watch the Animal Channel."

And he walked over to the entertainment center and opened the doors.

Reunited

Imagine riding in a car that propelled itself by scraping a giant metal squeegee along an endless track of chalkboard. Now imagine going to a NASCAR race where there were eight of these screeching cars competing against each other and maybe one guy on a big tricycle wearing a giant diaper.

What a horrible, terrible noise. I wouldn't care if that kind of car had really comfortable seats and a dashboard drink holder big enough for my big four-liter Halt'n'Buy Thunder-Guzzler. I would get out of that car. I would leave that race and that noise. I would go to a room where there were only sheep, pillows, and macramé. And there I would do mathematical problems until I could breathe normally again.

Well, this is kind of how Katie felt, being led through the rocky passes by a man who screamed constantly. *Constantly.*

Her nerves were tired. She felt like people had been drumming all over her skin for hours. She felt like she hadn't slept for days, and she wouldn't sleep for many more.

And he just kept right on striding along, tripping over rocks, yelping, howling, beeping, screeching, ululating, growling, keening, and once, tintinnabulating. This meant that he sang "DING DONG DING DONG. DING DONG DING DONG" in a voice that resembled the doorbell at the mansion of a South American dictator.

"Are we getting close?" she asked.

"Oh, I think we are," he said.

"Then could you stop screaming?"

"Could you stop looking? Could you stop using your eyes?"

"Would you cut it out?" said Katie, finally being rude to her elders. "My friend is in danger!"

"I cannot cut it out."

"You're not even blind! You can see perfectly where you're going!"

"No one ever said I was blind. They said I was brilliant." He explained, "I wear the blacked-out glasses so I don't accidentally rely on my sight." He opened his lungs really wide. *"AYOO AYOO AYOO AYOO AYOO."*

"Can you please stop that?"

"I cannot. I follow the ways of the bat."

"We need to find my friend!"

"He is no friend of mine, if he does not appreciate the special qualities of my voice."

"How could anyone appreciate your voice? It is completely obnoxious."

"I will have you know," said Dr. Schmeltzer, "that I am a highly accomplished ventriloquist. I am not simply some hack. I can place my voice anywhere. I can—"

Ventriloquist? Katie thought . . . She remembered back to that afternoon on the porch . . . Something bothered her . . . She had never actually *seen* the thief . . . She had, in fact, heard the thief and then run into—

Dr. Schmeltzer let out a hideous scream.

"Okay," said Katie. "I am really tired of this."

Dr. Schmeltzer let out another hideous scream.

"That's it," she said.

But this time he wasn't screaming to locate himself. He was screaming to warn her of the ten pairs of glowing golden eyes that were staring at them from the woods.

PACK AND PLUCK

Wolves.

When you read about "eyes glowing yellow in the dark," you think that it's just a figure of speech. The truth is, however, that wolves' eyes do glow by reflecting back light, and therefore it is terrifying when you see them illuminated at night. Once I had a party where I invited only wolves. It was kind of a tea dance. I was young and didn't have many friends. The wolves wanted the party in the dark; I convinced them to have a single night-light on so I could make my way around the room and see whether they were laughing with me or at me.

Yowza, after about ten minutes of that—their eyes glowing yellow in the dark, the brown evil light glinting off their fangs and the porcelain teacups, the lace doilies hanging torn from their snaggy teeth—I agreed to turn the light off. It was just better not to see. After that the party improved, and they were real nice. One of them even gave me an extra tool set he had in his car.

So the wolves' eyes, as I was saying, glowed yellow in the dark. The wolves stared at Katie and Dr. Schmeltzer. Dr. Schmeltzer and Katie stared at the wolves, which, in Dr. Schmeltzer's case, meant he screamed continuously.

And then the wolves started running.

Loping, really. They leaped and ran with a long-legged, rangy kind of gait.

Right into the forest.

Away from the screaming man, who terrified them.

Katie shone the light into the pine wood where the wolves had been circling.

There she saw a slouch-shouldered form.

Jasper Dash, Boy Technonaut.

She ran forward and he ran forward and she threw her arms around him. He would have thrown his arms around her, except that they were tied behind him. His face was covered with dirt and tracks of dried mucus.

She had never been happier to see a face in her life.

"Oh—Jasper—I'm so glad to see you!"

She turned him around and, putting the flashlight on the ground, began to work at the knots on his wrists.

"It seems a shame," said Dr. Schmeltzer, watching her, "to undo all that work when someone went to the trouble of tying it. Who's to say that you won't just need to tie him up again?"

Katie shot Dr. Schmeltzer a dirty glance.

Jasper's ropes fell to the ground. He sighed with pleasure and swung his arms in the air. He chafed his wrists.

"Katie," said Jasper, "I cannot even list the deuced awful things that have happened to me this afternoon." He took her hands. "Thank you for finding me. Thank you."

"Well, all's well that ends well," said Dr. Schmeltzer. "Let us now proceed posthaste to the cave. I shall scream loudly and incessantly to guide you."

Katie was angry now. She said, "It almost seems like you're *trying* to get us caught."

"Young lady, that is the most—"

But he did not finish his sentence, as he had seen a pair of glowing eyes looking at him out of the woods. The wolves were back, watching carefully, and braver. No scream would deter them now.

The three humans stood stock-still for a moment.

Wind picked up on the mountain, driven with the night. The pines around them surged.

"Let's go, chums!" exclaimed Jasper, and at the same moment, Katie ran forward to grab Dr. Schmeltzer's arm. Katie on one side, Jasper on the other, they began to tug him back toward the lodge. The wolves watched behind them.

Dr. Schmeltzer began his screaming again.

More wolves, alerted by the noise, slipped toward them through the wood.

The pine branches swayed in the wind.

Jasper saw gray bodies darting through the hemlocks.

Dr. Schmeltzer yelled.

Jasper pulled the old snotty duct tape out of his pocket. He hesitated. Katie saw what Jasper had, grabbed it out of his hand, and shoved it over Dr. Schmeltzer's mouth. Dr. Schmeltzer shook his head and protested. But soon he just mumbled.

"I'm sorry, sir," said Jasper. "It's for your own safety." They dragged him along the path.

As they stumbled forward, Jasper asked the professor, "Do you have any allergies we should know about? Grass, trees, flowers?" The professor shook his head. "Cats, dogs, mold, dust mites, ragwort, ragweed? . . . Do you have any history of asthma in your family? . . ."

They disappeared down the path.

On the mountain the temperature dropped. Wind came in from the north. The woods rattled with it.

A storm was brewing.

Eddie Wax Melts

Eddie Wax stared in shock at Lily, who was curled up in his entertainment center.

She looked him in the eye. She said, "You didn't do it, did you?"

He didn't know what to say. He was flabbergasted. He stared for a minute; then he started laughing. He said, "If it ain't Lily Gefelty, audio-visual component."

She swung her cramped arms out and began to unfold. She held on to the shelf and tried to crawl out. He gave her a hand. Her leg was stuck. He had to shove her back into the cabinet first and then help lift her out.

She stood up in front of him. "You didn't kidnap the Quints, did you?"

"Course I didn't kidnap the Quints," he said.

"You didn't steal the necklace, either."

"Lily, I thought we was friends."

"You've been stealing the stuffed animal heads from the lobby, though, haven't you?"

"The word is 'liberating.' I been freeing them to run in the wild and snarf their own food."

Lily looked at him sadly. "You're really upset about Stumpy, aren't you? You've never gotten over her."

"What's to get over?" he said defiantly. And then he stopped and sat down on the bed. He leaned forward and put his elbows on his knees; his head slumped. "People say she's gone, but I feel her all the time with me. At night my heart races along, going faster and faster, and it's also her heart, and even though I'm lying in bed, our heart is galloping. It's us going flying over the beaches, and there's wild grasses under her hoofs, and I can feel the lather all over me. Or during the day, sometimes I'm in town and it's all cars and gas stations and the music in the Piggly Wiggly and the Burger King, but all I can hear is the sound of her flying across the cliffs. We're charting unexplored countries. We're finding gold." Tears were running down his face. "We're having our series. We're having adventure after adventure, and nothing ever changes. We're always together."

Lily went over and sat next to him and put her hand on his arm.

She knew it was a good time not to say anything. Sometimes sadness is beyond words, because it is not an idea but a sensation, like hunger or pain.

And Eddie Wax, unspeaking, cried for all he wished were true.

Um, Hello?

It appears that people have somewhat forgotten about the Quints, with everything else that has been happening.

Don't think that the Quints didn't realize this.

"Um," said La. "Isn't someone supposed to come and check on us?"

"It would be really nice if we had a lamp or a bonfire."

"I'd like a mailbox," said one, "so I could keep getting postcards."

They waited for something to happen.

Against Injustice!

Katie, Jasper, and the gagged bat specialist made their way down toward the lodge. The wind was howling in the crags now. The trees shrugged and waved their arms.

Katie and Jasper, on either side of the duct-taped professor, exchanged glances in the bobbing glare from the flashlight. It was good to be back together again. They almost smiled.

They knew that now that they were reunited, nothing could stand in their way. They had encountered some awful things in their time—and yes, by awful things I mean tentacled things, sweating chloroform and hungry for subway cars—but nothing had ever defeated them; nothing, as Jasper saw it, had ever stood for long in the way of justice, truth, and kindness.

Go then, Jasper and Katie, back to your friend Lily, who awaits you. Steel your courage. Prepare to fight evil and injustice. Rush down the mountain while the storm gathers—and I wish you luck. We need more like you.

Though Dr. Schmeltzer, whose mouth has been duct-taped, would not necessarily agree.

PERSONAL SONS

Lily and Eddie Wax went down to the game room. The game-room walls were spiky with antlers. Antlers came out of the stone chimney and the window frames and the doors. People were playing cards there and billiards, sitting delicately to avoid getting poked.

Lily was worried. She said, "I wonder whether Katie and Dr. Schmeltzer found Jasper yet. Maybe we should go out after them."

They looked around the room.

The Manley Boys were shaking the billiard table as if they thought it was a pinball machine. They picked it up and rocked it.

While they played, they narrated tales of their success.

One said, "The Manley Boys—stout, fearless sons of ace detective Bark Manley—were good at all kinds of sports and games."

"They were playing billiards at the Moose Tongue Lodge one night," said Fud, shaking the billiard table. " 'Fud,' said Jank, 'we are the springy, up-to-the-minute sons of ace detective Bark Manley.' "

" 'Yes, Jank,' said Fud, the more wicker of the two," said Jank. " 'I wonder if there is a mystery here that we can solve with our powers of mystery. Solving.' "

" 'What about those missing Hooper Quints?' said Fud," said Jank. " 'That is surely a swell mystery that is equal to us, the standing, beaded, personal sons of ace detective Bark Manley.' His more attractive brother Jank agreed."

"His more attractive brother Jank did not agree. Jank was stupid."

"Fud Manley, other son of ace detective Bark Manley, was stupider."

They put down the billiard table. Growling, they faced each other.

Their confusing argument went on for a

while—"Jank was stupider"; "No, um, Fud was stupider"—until they started wrestling, a big thumping mess of cardigan sweaters and gray flannel trousers.

"Lily," said a woman Lily had never seen before, standing right next to her. "Good to see you!"

Lily looked at her suspiciously. "Hi . . . ," said Lily uncertainly.

"It's me," said the woman.

She was about forty-five, with long red hair. Lily had never seen her before in her life. "It's me," the woman repeated.

When Lily didn't say anything, the woman said, "They can make bamboo into anything these days. Check out this wristwatch!" She held out her wrist. It had a bamboo band. "That's pure bamboo!"

Lily was starting to feel like the earth had dropped away beneath her feet and she was someplace else.

"Why are you looking at me like a fish?" said the woman. "It's me, Lily."

Lily said, "I'm . . . I forgot your name."

The woman chucked Lily on the shoulder. "Remember my extrasensory perception? Most people do! You and me were always in the same search party!" She smiled wide. "And there's little Eddie Wax!"

Eddie looked at their new friend suspiciously.

Lily backed away, inspecting the woman through her bangs. "I don't remember you," said Lily.

The woman laughed and shrugged. "It's Rick," she said. "Rick. Remember? Oh, I got my green poplin jumpsuit all dirty."

Rick had worn a green poplin jumpsuit. The woman was wearing a red striped jacket. She did not look anything like Rick.

"I've got to go," said Lily. "I think I need some fresh air."

"Good to see you, Lily," said the woman. "I hope that everything turns out to be a wonderful success."

Lily walked quickly for the exit, feeling as

though she was going to throw up. Eddie ran along behind her.

They stepped outside onto one of the porches. The wind blew up from the chasms below them and hissed across the parking lot.

"That made no sense," said Lily. "I feel like I have a fever."

"Don't worry, Lily," said Eddie Wax. "We'll get to the bottom of this."

And I certainly hope he's right.

Eddie Wax and Lily stared, tense with confusion, into the dark night. Guests walked by lit windows. The trees *whoosh*ed in the chilly winds.

By the service entrance, a truck unloaded crates of red herrings for the kitchen.

There were about ninety-five pounds in all.

THE TRIO TOGETHER AGAIN

The life of a manager at a luxury hotel is never easy. One person complains that their room is too hot. Another complains that their room has too many angles. Another person thinks something is hidden inside their pillow. Someone else wants free shoes. A rock star keeps throwing an Etch A Sketch out the window and lighting his pajamas on fire. There are rats in the cellars. Huge rats. They want a cable connection.

And, then, in comes a girl and a boy holding one of the guests gagged between them, whispering that they've solved the mystery of the missing Hooper Quints. Even though the boy is Jasper Dash, famed for his escapades with riveted airships, and the girl is Katie Mulligan, known for combating evil wherever it shambles and drools, it is not easy to call together everyone in the hotel in one place and make accusations just because two thirteen-year-olds have requested it.

"I'm sorry," said Sid. "You'll have to wait an hour and a half until our evening Hot Cocoa Splurge in the game room."

"It's really important," said Katie. "We think we know everything we need to solve the crimes!"

"Wait for the Splurge," said Sid, and picked up an incoming phone call.

Katie and Jasper pulled the duct tape off Dr. Schmeltzer's face.

"Ow!" he said. "I believe you devilish tots have pulled out the fine crop of hairs I was cultivating on my nose."

"Oops," said Katie. "Sorry."

"Why, Dr. Schmeltzer," called Mrs. Mandrake from across the room, "look at you! Without those ugly hairs, you cut quite a dashing figure! Plucked, you remind me less of someone hiding behind a stand of Spanish moss."

"The bats, madam, do not shun hair on their snouts. They find hair beautiful."

"I admire your commitment," said Mrs. Mandrake. "Would you have any interest in sipping a cup of chocolate with me a little later, at the Cocoa Splurge?"

Dr. Schmeltzer considered.

"Katie! Jasper!" Lily called. She had just come out of the elevator, dressed in her coat. "I was about to go and look for you!"

Katie ran to her side. "We've got to talk," she said. "Lots and lots and lots to tell you. And we have to tell everything to Jasper. And we have to be *absolutely* sure who committed these crimes by an hour and a half from now." She looked around carefully to make sure no one had heard her.

"We're going to make our accusations at the Cocoa Splurge?"

Katie nodded. "Sid told us to."

Jasper came over, and Lily almost danced up and down to see him.

"You, Lily, are a sight for sore eyes," he said.

Now they were all three together again. Now everything felt right.

They rushed up to their room: That is, they rushed up to 46B, knocked loudly, and when the man wearily let them in, they rushed past him into his bathroom. Lily gave him a bag of lemon cookies she'd found.

They went into the Sky Suite and closed the door. Then they started babbling. No one knew who should speak first. They kept jabbering and pointing and laughing just for the sheer joy of being reunited.

Lily told them about the weird woman in the game room. Katie told them about what she had heard during the theft. Jasper told them about the dastardly mucus.

"Mucus?!?" said Lily.

"Snot," said Katie, wriggling her hands. "I saw it. It was *ewww.*"

"That was one of the closest scrapes with death I've ever had," said Jasper, "and it happened mostly in my sinuses."

Pretty soon they realized that they were going to have to organize their various clues. Jasper ran to a riveted desk and pulled out some Post-it notes.

They started to write down all the things they had learned about the mystery.

I wish I had done that, too. Frankly, I am becoming increasingly worried that it is impossible to find a solution to this puzzle that works. Then I will be in big trouble. You will seek me out, and you will yell at me while I'm trying to eat my luncheon special in peace. I will snivel into my pad thai.

I may be in trouble here.

We will have to see.

As they stuck the Post-it notes on the walls in rows, Katie and Lily and Jasper asked each other questions like these: Did the person who stole the necklace also kidnap the Quints? Was there just one person, or were there several people involved? How did the kidnapping tie in with the theft? Was it likely that one of the guests was the person in the black ski mask at the cave? Was there any way to prove their suspicions beyond a reasonable doubt? And do it in time for the Cocoa Splurge?

Katie was enjoying solving mysteries again. Her eyes were bright and she kept licking her lips.

"Opportunity," said Jasper. "Who had the opportunity to kidnap the Quints?"

"Almost anyone," said Lily. "The kidnapping happened before everyone gathered at the hotel."

"We met everyone after the kidnapping happened," said Katie.

"Who had the opportunity to steal the necklace?" mused Lily.

"It happened when you were all gathered on the lawn in your search parties, about ready to start up the mountain," said Katie.

"The necklace was stolen while people . . ." Jasper stalled. He blushed. He did not think it was proper to mention people going to the bath-room in the presence of girls.

"Used the bathroom," said Katie. "Who went to the bathroom right then?"

"A lot of the guests," said Jasper.

"But not Rick," Lily noted. "He was with me. And we should remember, it doesn't have to be a guest." She blew her bangs back from her face. "It could be a person from the staff. Like Sid."

"Good point," said Katie. "Suspect every-one."

This kind of discussion continued for a while. They were thinking and arguing and bringing up points and counterpoints. And gradually things became clear to them. They scribbled out more clues. Soon they had Post-it notes all over the wall, and Katie had also stuck some on Jasper, who was sitting in the way, stroking his chin. He got feisty and stuck three motives on her back when she wasn't looking.

Lily pulled them off and showed them to her.

Katie tickled Jasper when he was writing a note about Mrs. Mandrake, so it read:

First missed necklace when a ⌒

Outside, the air had turned frigid. The windows of the lodge slowly glazed white. Snow started to fall over the black, twisted places in the forest.

Up on the tallest peak, a scientist who lived in an antenna went out, held his thumbs to the wind, and went back inside to make a warm radioactive fire and read a storybook on benzene rings.

And in the cave?

The cave was empty.

Both rooms.

The hour of the Splurge—and of accusations—grew closer.

INTRIGUED BY THE SPLURGE

Everyone was intrigued by the Splurge. Usually, the only thrill with the Splurge was the popcorn bar and occasionally a few college students who had gotten tangled playing Twister and who couldn't get unbunched. They had to be hand-fed the popcorn by bellhops.

But tonight there was mystery. There was accusation. Everyone had heard about it.

People got there early for seats.

There, on one of the sofas, was Rick reading *Road & Track* magazine. There was Mrs. Mandrake, her hair piled high atop her head and clasped with a huge amber comb, talking with Dr. Schmeltzer, who was wearing a black velvet evening jacket and felt tufts on his ears. There was Eddie Wax trading gymnastics stories with

the water polo team. There were the Cutesy Dell
Twins, admiring the wooden construction of the
roof eaves ("Nice joinery!"). There were the
Manley Boys, chalking the billiard balls. There
were Dix Wickerbasket and His Amazing Dix-
Chords, striking a pose where they all looked in
different directions. One of them ran to get their
singer more cocoa, then more marshmallows,
then more caramel corn, then more cocoa again.

And there were our three nervous heroes,
Jasper, Katie, and Lily, huddled together near
the door, hoping against hope that they were
right in their deductions.

Everyone in the room murmured. Everyone
watched each other with a delighted kind of
suspicion. Everyone seemed very thrilling and
mysterious. Lily and Katie, looking around the
room, realized that the more boring someone
looked, the easier it was to imagine some amazing and fascinating criminal past they were trying to hide. A gray husband and wife who had
run out of things to say to each other twelve
years before might really be brother and sister

safecrackers contemplating crimes. A busi-
nessman might be selling land that was
deep underwater. A man in a mall-store
sweater and track shoes might
smuggle endangered animals
across the Canadian border.
Narwhals, for example.

Lily and Katie
whispered unlikely
crimes to each other.
It helped them forget their stage fright.

If they were wrong, they were in big trouble.

Big, big, BIG trouble.*

Dix Wickerbasket's band, bored, began to
whistle "Begin the Beguine."

The Manley Boys sat down and waited for
some action.

"Hey," someone said loudly. "I wonder if

---

*Does the larger type help you? (A) Yes. (B) No. (C) It saddens me. You,
sir, are tawdry.

anyone would like to make, I don't know, any *accusations* tonight."

"That would be great," said someone else. "We would listen real close."

Everyone fell silent and stared at our heroic trio.

"Miss Mulligan," said Sid, "I think people are wondering if you can shed any light upon this mystery."

Katie looked at the faces before her, faces turned to observe the drama, people waiting to hear what she had to say. Yes, she was terrified and her heart beat quickly. But also, she felt the thrill of conclusion—for soon, she and Lily and Jasper would put things right. Katie wouldn't have missed this moment for anything. It could turn out that her theory was wrong; she hoped it was not. Either way, the next few minutes would be crucial. Eventful. Thrilling.

Katie cleared her throat. She stepped forward.

At that, there was a hideous scream.

Elementary!

"Sorry," said Dr. Schmeltzer. "I was just looking for one of those little sugar packets."

Katie, putting her hand on her heart to still it, calmed herself.

And she began.

"There are several mysteries here at the hotel," she said. "First of all, there is the question of why the animal heads in the lobby keep disappearing and reappearing in the woods. Then there is the missing necklace. Then, most importantly, there is the disappearance of the Hooper Quints."

"Who still," someone pointed out, "are out there somewhere."

"Exactly," said Katie. "It turns out, though,

that not all of those things are connected. For example, the animal heads were being . . . um . . ."

"Liberated," Lily supplied.

". . . *liberated*," continued Katie, "by a guest whose beloved pet had been stuffed years ago. He didn't have anything to do with the other crimes."

Katie paused and looked carefully from face to face. She said, "For a long time tonight, I thought about who might have stolen the necklace. I was right nearby when the necklace was stolen, so I had the most evidence of who the thief was. Here's what happened: I heard someone talking to himself as he searched Mrs. Mandrake's room. Just afterward, Dr. Schmeltzer appeared. He stumbled across me. I might have been more suspicious of him, except that I heard the thief run by while we were talking.

"I *heard* the thief," Katie emphasized. "I didn't see him! Later on this made me suspicious — when I discovered that Dr. Schmeltzer *is a ventriloquist*. He could alter his voice to sound like someone else—and he could throw his voice to sound like someone running away, even while he stood right near me."

People gasped and looked at Dr. Schmeltzer.

"As a ventriloquist, Dr. Schmeltzer could have stolen the necklace and then imitated Rick's voice to remove suspicion from himself."

"I am innocent," said the bat specialist with dignity. "You may burn me upon a pyre, and still I will protest: I am innocent."

"He *could* have stolen the necklace," said Katie, "BUT I don't think he did. Not any-more!"

Her hands were trembling. If she was wrong, it would be a disaster. She and Lily and Jasper were just guessing, after all.

She caught the eyes of the Cutesy Dell Twins, and suddenly she felt even more nervous. They were watching her carefully to see what she would say next.

And then suddenly, one of them whispered, "Go on, Katie. You're doing real good so far."

And Katie drew a deep breath and went on.

"Okay ... So ... After several confusing things happened today, Jasper, Lily, and me talked about who had kidnapped the Quints. We just couldn't figure it out. Nothing made sense. Until suddenly we realized ... What if the Quints *were never kidnapped at all*?"

Now everyone was bewildered.

"No one here has ever read any of the Quints' books," said Katie. "No one knows what they look like. It's been years since their series came out. In that time, what if they've aged? What if they were full-grown adults now? What if they were jealous of other people who have appeared in books, and they wanted to show us all that they were still a force to be reckoned with? What if they decided to *stage a crime,* therefore, so they could solve it? What if they *pretended to be kidnapped and then stole something important, so that when they pretended to free themselves and saved the priceless necklace, everyone would be impressed?*"

"Yeah?" said one of the Manley Boys. "What if?"

"Here's how they could do it," said Katie. "One of them could be out on a search party, very loud and very visible. Meanwhile, another Quint could walk into the hotel, *pretending to be the same man,* and, without anyone noticing, go right up to Mrs. Mandrake's room, break in, and steal the necklace. The other Quints could be hidden up at a secret cave.

"Then that would be the perfect alibi. No one would suspect that person of stealing anything. If anyone saw him or heard him while he searched for the necklace and then accused him, he could easily say that he was part of a search party all afternoon . . . Couldn't he, *Rick?*"

Rick put down his magazine. "Question for me?" he said.

Katie repeated, "Couldn't you? . . . Rick?"

"Could I what?"

Katie shuffled her hand in the air. "Be a Quint. Whose brother impersonated you while you were out searching with Lily and Mrs. Mandrake. So he could steal the Mandrake Necklace and you could have an alibi. And that way you could regain your former glory."

"That's the stupidest plot I've ever heard," said Rick. "And you have nothing to prove it."

Now people were looking suspiciously back at Katie, Lily, and Jasper.

Jasper stepped forward. "But we do. Luckily for us, those cunning Quints made one fatal mistake." He paused briefly for dramatic effect. "*They never realized that they are fraternal, not identical, siblings!* That is to say, they do not all look the same."

"In fact," said Lily, "some of them are women and some of them are men. This is how we figured out what was happening: That lady there came up to me, pretending to be her brother who had been in my search party. She thought she looked just like him, and that I'd never tell the difference."

"We suspect," said Jasper, "that when they were kids, their nun nurse lied to them about being identical—as she did about their musical ability."

The woman rose. "This is ridiculous!" she cried. "I have never heard a more silly story in my whole life!"

"Several Quints were pretending to be one," said Katie. "This is why I thought I heard Rick's voice when the necklace was stolen. I *did* hear his voice — or, to be more exact, the voice of his one identical brother."

"This is the stupidest idea I've ever heard," said Rick.

One of the Cutesy Dell Twins rolled her eyes. "Duh, it's *your* plan, not Katie's," she said.

"Yeah," said the other Twin. "It's not her fault your plan is lame. Stop being this total jerk about it."

"Earlier tonight," said Lily, "that woman there introduced herself to me as 'Rick,' the false name her brother had chosen. But first she kept on saying 'It's me!' . . ."

"Remember," added Jasper, "the Quints were all nicknamed after the names of the notes of the musical scale."

Lily explained, "Katie and I know from our piano lessons—"

"—and I know," said Jasper, "from my theremin lessons—"

"—that the notes of the scale begin *Do, Re, Mi.* What she was really saying was 'It's Mi,' which is the nickname her brothers and sisters call her."

At that, "Rick"—actually Fa Hooper—rose, throwing his magazine to the rug. He stood with his fists in balls. As he looked around the room, his lips twitched, as if he wanted to devour them all and lick his lips clean of them.

"You'll never catch us," he said. And he cried, "*QUICKLY!*" to his sister—and grabbed her arm. She took his hands and they spun around.

People veered away from them, spilling hot chocolate on the floor.

Mi and Fa came to a rest and smiled triumphantly, side by side.

"There!" crowed Fa. "Shoot if you will, fools! But now you have no idea which one of us is which! You'll never know which one of us is the *real* Mi and which one is the man you know as Rick!"

He spread his arms wide.

"Ha-ha!" he said. "Ha-ho-ho, you fools! Now try to tell reality from illusion!" He crossed his arms and grinned like an emperor.

Everyone was embarrassed.

People shifted from foot to foot. People cleared their throats. A few people watched but licked the inside of their cocoa cups.

"Um," explained Katie apologetically, "first of all, you really don't look anything alike."

"And second of all," said Lily, "you're dressed differently. One of you is wearing a skirt."

"And third of all," said Jasper, "you are both dastardly criminals in any case, so we could just arrest both of you."

Rick/Fa looked panicked. He yelled, "Okay! Brothers, sisters, unite!"

Suddenly the glass doors to the porch rattled

and were kicked open. Panes shattered. People screamed.

In ran three more Quints—two men and a woman—dressed painfully in undersized linoleum lederhosen and carrying guns.

Everyone was held at pistol point.

"Okay," said Rick/Fa. "So the little brats are right. For years we've been forgotten. Oh, I used to have golden hair, and now it's gray. Yes, I used to have apple cheeks and shiny shorts. Now—all *tarnished.* So we invited you people here with those fake coupons so you could witness our big comeback.

"Tonight," he said, "was to be our victory night. We were going to dress up as our child selves and return here and claim our reward for finding the necklace—and publicize our fearless escape from the imaginary kidnappers. But these kids, these stupid, irritating kids, ruined that plan. The young ruin everything for the aging. That's how the world works. But there are other ways for us to win this little game. We will turn this Cocoa Splurge into the greatest robbery the world has ever known." He walked among the guests, holding a gun. "People, take off your jewelry. Hand it to me. We will add it to *this* priceless little item . . ."

He pointed at his brother. His brother reached into his pocket and pulled out the Mandrake Necklace. It glittered in the light. People *ooh*ed and *aah*ed.

"*That's* what you stole?" asked Mrs. Mandrake.

"Yes, of course, you old fool," said Fa.

"I wish you wouldn't call me an old fool," said Mrs. Mandrake. "Especially when I told you that I took precautions to secure my necklace. That piece of glittering gimcrackery isn't the necklace at all."

"What?!?" growled Fa.

"No, for safety's sake, I had the real Mandrake Necklace ground up into little pieces."

"So you . . . what?!? We didn't steal the necklace?"

"No, darling. You stole the copy I had hidden to mislead the stupider of thieves."

"So where is the real thing?" he said. He walked over to her and jabbed the gun into her temple. "Tell me where it is!"

"As you well know, I haven't the faintest idea. The granulated necklace was stolen. I had it hidden inside a pepper shaker."

Jasper blinked, blushed, and made sure he didn't look down at his waist, where the pepper shaker was shoved between his belt loops.

"Earlier today, down in the lobby," said Mrs. Mandrake, "some miserable thief switched the pepper shaker for a flashlight."

Gingerly, Jasper stepped to the side and concealed his midriff behind an overstuffed chair.

Fa was crazed with anger. Snarling, shaking Mrs. Mandrake's arm, he demanded, *Tell me where that necklace is, you rich old bat, or the next society dinner you'll attend will be with Saint Peter and all the angels!*

There was a click as he prepared to shoot.

Everything Falls into Place
(with a Thumping Noise)

Salvation came from an unexpected direction.

One of the Cutesy Dell Twins grabbed a billiard ball and hurled it at Fa.

It clocked him on the forehead and he stumbled backward, clutching at his brow.

And one of the water polo players caught the ball on the rebound and hurled it at another Quint. It bonked her on the side of the skull, and she wobbled and started to fall.

Fa grabbed at Lily's shoulder to steady himself. She stepped out of the way. He fell backward at her feet.

Meanwhile, Katie had caught the billiard ball, and she threw it at another Quint—who ducked, rammed his head on a pair of moose

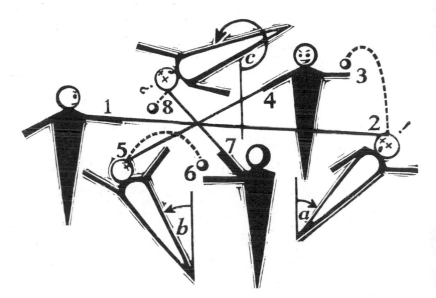

antlers, and with a wooden *plok* was knocked unconscious.

I am bad at action scenes and even worse at counting. Have I knocked out all the Quints yet? If there are any left in the room (and I'm pretty sure there are), they had a coughing spell and Jasper bopped them with the pepper grinder.

"Hooray!" said Fud Manley. "We did it!"

"No—watch out!" said Lily. "There's another one!"

"I think that's five," said Sid. "One, two, three, four—"

"There are six," said Katie. "Doe, Ray, Mi, Fa, Sol, and La!"

"That's right," said Sol, stepping into the room, gun raised.

Six Quints! How had Katie, Lily, and Jasper figured out there were actually *six* Quintuplets? Well, at first they realized that there had to be someone other than the five Quints involved to pretend to be a kidnapper when the taxicab was held up.

Then the three of them had started to think about the Quints' names, which were all the names of the musical notes. In the book Sid had read from—*The Hooper Quints on an Oil Derrick; or, The Danger Gang!*—it mentioned Quints named for the musical scale from Doe to La—which meant *Do, Re, Mi, Fa, Sol, La*—*six* notes, not five! This meant six Quints! Astonishing. Just the kind of surprising twist that makes a mystery novel particularly satisfying. Once again—this time in the question of numbers—the Hooper Quintuplets had been cruelly misled by their nun nanny.

So, see? Six. It all works out completely logically. Did you doubt me?

Now, as a result of this mathemato-musical confusion, the whole roomful of guests was in a pickle. Sol Hooper held them all at gunpoint.

Sol looked just like Fa. He, however, was dressed in black.

"Suffering solfège," muttered Jasper Dash. "This is not a pretty picture."

"Give up," said Lily. "We have all your brothers and sisters."

"And you don't have the Mandrake Necklace," said Katie. "Mrs. Mandrake ground it up so that no one would be able to find it."

Sol, blinking rapidly, aimed again at Mrs. Mandrake, howling with rage.

She saw the barrel swinging her way and screamed.

Eddie Wax jumped from a table onto Sol and yanked at the man's arms. The two of them bumbled around the room, knocking into antlers—their struggle punctuated with *Ow*s and *Yikes*es and *Ouch*es as they were jabbed from all sides.

Eddie Wax grabbed at Sol's gun.

Shots rang out—people shrieked—and plaster drifted from the ceiling.

Eddie finally got his hands firmly around the pistol—he pried it from the man's hands.

Lily and Katie were at Sol's sides, pulling on his shirt, trying to knock him so he would let go of Eddie.

Sol, full of rage, caught a glimpse of a huge, pointy rack of caribou antlers.

Leaning forward, he ran straight toward them—trying to skewer Eddie on the biggest spikes.

Katie screamed—and she and Lily punched at the Quint—but he shoved his hand into Lily's face and sent her sprawling. Katie tripped on Doe—she fell—

Sol threw himself and the freckled boy jockey toward the sharp horns, growling—

And something came between him and the spikes.

Something invisible.

Sol staggered backward.

"No!" commanded Jasper. "Stop, you scoundrel!"

The sharp prongs of the antlers glinted in the light. Eddie wailed for mercy.

Sol ran forward again.

And once again came up against a shape in the air.

A shape hot with transparent anger and lather.

Sol started to sense that he was up against something that was not of this world.

He backed up carefully.

Eddie let go of Sol. He slipped to the ground and watched the empty place in front of them. . . . His face was full of hope.

A shape solidified there.

Two glowing eyes.

A mane of shadow.

Eddie's breath was sudden and delighted.

It was the ghost of Stumpy.

Sol fired at it—but of course the bullets did nothing.

The spirit horse whinnied, reared up on its hind legs, and wheeled its hoofs in the air.

Sol panicked and fired again, sending the chandelier rocking, firing as many times as he could, sinking backward away from the flailing hoofs.

The phantom horse let out a weird, angry howl.

Sol, terrified, fell down before it. He had run out of bullets.

With a cataclysmic thump of ghostly hoofs, the horse landed and placed a heavy foot on Sol's chest.

Eddie ran to the horse, calling, "Stumpy! Stumpy, girl!"

The horse bashfully removed her hoof from the criminal and greeted her rider with a whicker.

Lily and Katie ran forward and grabbed Sol's arms. Jasper and the Manley Boys grabbed his double, Fa, who was lying, tongue out, on the floor.

"Stumpy," said Eddie Wax, rubbing his dead horse's neck. "Good old Stumpy."

The ghost horse leaned her head against Eddie's chest.

Everyone watched the beautiful reunion of horse and boy.

The boy went to the refreshment table and picked up an empty, torn sugar packet. He mimed pouring sugar into his hand. The horse licked his empty palm of nonexistent sugar, and the boy laughed.

Eddie Wax had found his horse.

They were together again.

He pulled himself up onto Stumpy's back. Everyone clapped.

"Thank you," said Eddie Wax. "We're leaving now."

"No," said Lily, "thank *you*. And thank Stumpy."

Eddie whispered into the horse's ear.

Outside, snow blew across the porch and the parking lot. Eddie Wax and his phantom steed headed into the darkness, picking up speed—lifting off—flying through the air.

People ran after them as they galloped toward the clouds.

There they were, the white ghost mare and her boy, headed at last for immortality.

Katie and Lily, without even having to talk about it, both started singing, in haunting, small voices:

"Yippee-eye-oh! Yippee-eye-ay!"

And the Cutesy Dell Twins joined in, singing softly together, *"Ghost riders in the sky . . ."*

And so Eddie Wax was reunited with the horse he loved; and they rode through the clouds, outpacing Pestilence, Famine, Death, and War; and they rode through the gulches where flames billowed hotly and the fields of green where the asphodel flowers never wither. At night they slept in the prairies on the dark side of the moon, and Eddie Wax told his horse tales by the fire,

occasionally throwing more oxygen on the flame to keep it burning. They followed the aurora borealis and clattered down the rings of Saturn and they herded asteroids, and their adventures have not yet come to an end.

When Eddie and his horse had disappeared, people went back inside.

"Mrs. Mandrake," said Jasper. "I believe that I accidentally recovered the Granulated Necklace." He presented her with the pepper grinder. "It was not a theft, but a misunderstanding. I am honor-bound to report that Fud Manley, well-built son of ace detective Bark Manley, switched the pepper grinder and his flashlight without realizing his mistake."

He guiltily realized that the time had come to admit that he had snorted some of the granulated gemstones up his nose, trying to sneeze. "And I . . . Mrs. Mandrake, when tied to a chair and attacked by a poisonous snake, I—"

"Oh, what a delightful boy you are," said Mrs. Mandrake. She took the grinder from him. "I've been feeling naked all evening. It is time to pepper my décolletage." She tilted her head to the side and began cranking the grinder. She generously applied diamond necklace to her shoulders and neck. "Here, darling," she said to Dr. Schmeltzer. "Could you sprinkle a bit on my nape?"

"I certainly could," said Dr. Schmeltzer. "I don't mind telling you that when I heard you called an 'old bat,' my heart began pounding. And your shriek, madam—you and I could get along very well, indeed."

Meanwhile, several of the hotel's maid service had tied up the Quints.

"I don't know why you're doing this," said Fa. "You don't have anything on us. We didn't kidnap anyone. And we didn't steal the necklace."

Katie said, "You did threaten us all with guns and try to steal a bunch of stuff and try to stab Eddie Wax with caribou horns."

"*Hmm,*" said Fa. "True."

"You rascal," said Jasper, "you did tape my mouth shut without making adequate inquiries as to whether I suffered from any plant-related allergies." He frowned. "Though that, I guess, is the least of your crimes."

"That was my brother," Fa said. "I think."

Lily asked, "What happened to your nun nanny? The one who told you that you could sing and that you were identical and that there were five of you?"

"Eh," said Fa. "It was a long time ago. She was a nun. She was a nanny. So we figured she could fly." He shook his head. "That was just the first in a long line of disappointments."

The snow fell more thickly around the grand hotel. Inside, through the frosted windows, people drank cocoa and hot toddies and ate Cajun-style popcorn. People stomped in from midnight sleigh rides, dusting snow off their coats and laughing. Everyone was happy suddenly to be alive.

In the grand lobby, the Dix-Chords struck up tunes and people danced. They jitterbugged and fox-trotted. Mrs. Mandrake and Dr. Schmeltzer spun each other and tipped their heads back and clasped each other by the arms. The Cutesy Dell Twins stood back to back, rocking their heads and holding their arms out straight. The three heroes of the evening danced together in a triangle—Jasper doing formal ballroom dances with an imaginary partner, Lily shuffling shyly from one side to the other, and Katie throwing herself around like a wacky hyena. The Manley Boys hurled popcorn at each other. Sid whistled the melody while the band's pianist accompanied him with punchy chords.

The bellhops got up on the counter and tap-danced on the blotters, while the water polo team, grinning widely, lined up on the staircase and toppled one by one into a fountain of champagne. They swam in kaleidoscopic formations around the trussed-up Hooper Quints, who lowed along with the song in awful close harmony, their heads bent together while popcorn rained down upon them; and around them, the water polo team enthusiastically circled and kicked and held up their hands making jazz fingers; and above them, chandeliers sparkled, and

animal eyes glittered from the mounted heads remaining, and corks flew through the air.

Finally, they all gathered around the tree and sang carols.

Sid, smiling widely, proclaimed, "Hooray! It's the best Christmas ever!"

People clapped.

"Um," said Katie. "Isn't it the middle of summer vacation?"

There was an awkward pause while the author checked his notes.

The water polo team clambered out of the fountain and toweled off the champagne.

Finally, a bellhop ran forward with a telegram in an envelope.

Sid tore open the envelope, read the message, and nodded.

"Hooray!" he proclaimed. "It's the best summer vacation ever!"

They gathered around the palm tree and sang summer songs while the wind blew down from the mountaintop and the snow gathered on the roof of the Moose Tongue Lodge and Resort.

SNOWFALL

Snow fell in spirals through the black trees. It landed on the mountain streams and disappeared. It lay on the burrows of wolves. As night grew deeper, clouds snagged on the summit, on the antennae there, and everything was silenced.

Snow fell on crags and on pines. Secretly, it muffled shapes and finished them.

It tumbled past the window where Lily and Katie knelt on Lily's bed, looking out at the darkness.

"The Hooper Quints' books were published a long time ago," whispered Katie. "Back in the 1930s or 1940s or '50s. Back when Jasper's books came out."

She could, somehow, feel that Lily was nodding, though the room was unlit.

"Then, why . . . ," started Katie, and she fell silent.

She tried again. "Then why did they get older and Jasper didn't?"

Lily reached out and laid her hand on the windowpane. It was cold to the touch. In the faint ghost of light from outside, the spaces between her fingers grew slips of fog.

She said, "I guess because no one read their books. So they were free. They could change and grow older. People somewhere must still read about Jasper. So he's still who he was."

Katie thought about this. She rocked onto her haunches. She said to her friend, "Is Jasper going to always stay the same, then?"

"I don't know," said Lily.

"What will happen," asked Katie, "what will happen if we get older and he stays the same?" Her voice caught in her throat. "If we're in college or married to people and he's still a kid?"

"I don't know," whispered Lily even softer.

They sat side by side without speaking. One room away Jasper slept, exhausted by his day, heavy with allergy medication. He breathed softly, his hair smeared across his forehead, his bed lumpy with the electrical parts he liked to study before he fell asleep.

"I don't want to leave him behind," said Lily.

Katie sighed. "He already is behind," she said. She faintly smiled. "It's kind of cute. Sometimes I have to remind him—'Hello, welcome to 1998!'"

Lily looked at her friend, startled. She could barely make out Katie's features.

"Katie," she said quietly. "It's not."

"Not...?"

"Nineteen ninety-eight. It's a lot later than that."

Time passed slowly in the room after Lily said this. It was marked by the thrumming of the furnace somewhere far below. Neither of them knew what to say.

Lily whispered, "Nineteen ninety-eight is when the Horror Hollow series came out."

Katie did not look at her friend for a while. She thought about what Lily had said. She drew her knees up against her chest and put her arms around her legs. "I'm stuck," said Katie. "I'll never grow up. And you will."

"We don't know what's going to happen," said Lily.

"Jasper and I won't change and you will. You'll be a mother."

"We're best friends. We'll always be," Lily insisted; but Katie didn't respond.

The wind picked up outside and they heard the hotel creaking. They looked at each other's faces in the dark.

"Let's wake him up," said Katie. "We'll play cards. All together."

"Let him sleep," said Lily. "Don't worry, Katie. We have years."

"Maybe," said Katie. She took Lily's hand. "Maybe we do."

They stared out the window, but all they could see now was their own faint reflection, their faces in the night, as if they hovered, ghost eyed, in the cold.

Snow fell over the mountain.

VELOCITY

The next day there were pancakes for everyone. There were waffles.

Jasper, Katie, and Lily tramped through the snow. They went over bridges and made their way through tall ravines. Their voices echoed. They went skiing with the Cutesy Dell Twins. The Twins taught Lily how to stay standing.

In the forest the snow flickered with light like mica. It fell in dust from the trees. Katie pulled on boughs to douse the others and they screamed. They pelted her with snowballs.

Katie and the Cutesy Dell Twins decided that they were going to dress up for dinner and get Lily to dress up, too, and they talked about it while they skied down the slopes. Katie could tell that Lily was kind of excited by the idea of seeing herself with her hair done up fancily.

Jasper, meanwhile, turned up the collar of his Strato-jac and went over jumps on his amazing subatomic rocket-sledge.

Dr. Schmeltzer and Mrs. Mandrake tobogganed down a slope together, screaming all the way. They went over a jump and whapped to a stop at the bottom, inches from a river.

"You, dearest, are a crazy man," howled Mrs. Mandrake happily.

"Darling, please don't call me that."

"Crazy?"

"A man. To the bats, I am a Long Ground-Mouse."

The water polo team and the Cutesy Dell Twins were getting very friendly at the bottom of the slope. The Manley Boys, miffed that they hadn't solved the case, were hiding each other's ski hats and pretending it was a crime.

Katie, standing on her skis, looked around her at all the people rising on the lift and shooting past her on the trail, the people laughing and skidding and jumping.

It is strange that everyone staying at the Lodge that weekend was so full of longing—for their youth, or their horse, or their fame, or their glitter, or perfect joinery, or night flight— so full of longing that they ended up a little broken somehow, unable to see what was obvious to others, unaware of what year they lived in, or how they looked, or what was right and wrong. We all are lost and confused in this way, so full of longing for things: This is why we need people who solve mysteries, whether they are the mysteries of bloodstains on the carpet, or the mysteries of space, or the mystery of who we are.

Of course, Katie didn't think these things. She was just thinking how grateful she was that people had let her do what she was good at. Other people could play in bands or paint or make things out of wood. She could solve crimes and fight off things that jumped out of bushes.

Remembering her tantrum at home on the garage floor, she was really glad she wasn't in that mood anymore. She was glad that everyone seemed happy now, even the Quints, who were all skiing down the mountain, tied in a clump, with police officers snowboarding alongside them.

And though she couldn't have put it into words, Katie was also thinking this: In this world, this confusion of motive, opportunity, and means, where everyone yearned to the point of blindness, where she herself didn't even know the year, where the solutions made no more sense than the questions—still there was the mountain, and there were people falling in love and families soaking each other with ice, and there were dogs playing tricks in the powder, and there were friends like Jasper and Lily.

These things were no more substantial than a phantom horse or a snowfall in July. But that was why she had to embrace it all so hard, with such joy.

Jasper waved up to her. Katie waved back.

She kicked off and skied toward him—right toward him—and didn't stop until she'd collided with him and Lily, and, together, the three of them lay aching and laughing and pummeling each other in the snow; and their skis were crossed like the swords of musketeers of old who pledged oaths of fealty, many daring escapades, rakish hats, and friendship eternal, come what may.

APPENDIX A
THE LONELIEST WHALE

The following article was sent to me by a reader:

> LONDON (Reuters)—A lone whale, with a voice unlike
> any other, has been wandering the Pacific for the past
> 12 years, American marine biologists said Wednesday.
>
> Using signals recorded by the U.S. Navy to track
> submarines, they traced the movement of whales in the
> northern Pacific and found that a lone whale singing
> at a frequency of around 52 hertz has cruised the
> ocean since 1992. Its calls, despite being clearly
> those of a baleen, do not match those of any known
> species of whale, which usually call at frequencies of
> between 15 and 20 hertz. The mammal does not follow
> the migration patterns of any other species either,
> according to team leader Mary Anne Daher. [Dec. 8, 2004]

Oh, to travel the dark whale-roads of the
earth with a song no one else sings, calling for a

mate who shall not find you, companions who do not sink or sound, save in your barnacled dreams. What could be lonelier than this whale, alone of its kind?

This book I dedicate to you.

Though you cannot read it, may you find joy in your own song and the friendship of crabs, and rhythm in the oscillation of kelp.

OFFICIAL COMPLAINT FORM AND STATIONERY FOR THE MOOSE TONGUE LODGE AND RESORT

(For use by young adventurers whose astounding lives often take them to a mountain setting where they encounter thrilling dissatisfactions)

Moose Tongue Lodge and Resort

ON SCENIC MT. ANDERSON

Complaint Form

We apologize that you have not been entirely satisfied with your stay at the Moose Tongue Lodge and Resort. We will do all we can to rectify the situation.

Please specify the nature of your complaint:

☐ Unhappy with Room   ☐ Unhappy with View   ☐ Unhappy with Life

☐ Gastric   ☐ Criminal   ☐ Geological

☐ Extraterrestrial   ☐ Extrasensory   ☐ Extra Cheese Sauce

☐ Spies   ☐ Personal Tragedy   ☐ Hereditary Insanity

☐ Automotive   ☐ Subaquatic   ☐ Undead/Unholy

☐ Athletic   ☐ Romantic   ☐ Lycanthropic

☐ Scatological   ☐ Eschatological   ☐ Could I Get Soup?

Details (attach extra sheets if necessary):

_____

_____

_____

_____

_____

_____

_____

_____

_____

_____

_____

_____

Would you like the concierge to order you a:

☐ Taxi   ☐ Aspirin   ☐ Master Detective

☐ Silver Bullet   ☐ Lead-lined Suit   ☐ Time Capsule

☐ Set of Fresh Towels   ☐ Magical Broadsword   ☐ Shaving Kit

☐ Counterspy   ☐ Bazooka   ☐ Shoe Shine

☐ Kid Wizard with a Divot in His Forehead   ☐ Soup

Greetings from the

Moose Tongue Lodge and Resort

ON SCENIC MT. ANDERSON

Jupiter's Moons!
Turn the page for a peek at the next
thrilling tale by M. T. Anderson.

IT IS A LAND OF WONDERS
IT IS A LAND OF MYSTERY
IT IS A LAND THAT TIME FORGOT
OR CHOSE SPECIFICALLY NOT TO REMEMBER

IT IS CALLED DELAWARE

Cut off from the civilized world for untold years by prohibitive interstate tolls at the New Jersey border, Delaware is nothing but a name to most of us, a place impossibly strange and exotic, a land of mountaintop monasteries wreathed in mist, steaming jungles where vines embrace the stone heads of fallen gods; it is a coast of golden bays where simple fisherfolk mend their nets while overhead pterodactyls flap home in the evening's afterglow.

It is into the heart of this forbidden realm—possibly the most thrilling and unusual of the mid-Atlantic states—that Jasper Dash, Boy Technonaut, and his friends Lily Gefelty and Katie Mulligan must travel to unravel a terrible mystery. Their journey will take them from the floor of their school gym, in the midst of an intramural stare-eyes competition, to the far reaches of the imagination. So sit back, readers! Let your hands clench, your jaw go slack, and your forehead break out in hives as you read the tale of . . .

JASPER DASH AND THE FLAME-PITS OF DELAWARE

The third installment of
M. T. Anderson's Thrilling Tales

*** Coming soon to a junk shop near you! ***